Other books by Erika Lopez

Lap Dancing for Mommy
Tender Stories of Disgust, Blame, and Inspiration

They Call me Mad Dog!

Flaming Iguanas

An Illustrated
All-Girl Road Novel
Thing

Erika Lopez

★

SCRIBNER PAPERBACK FICTION
PUBLISHED BY SIMON & SCHUSTER

SCRIBNER PAPERBACK FICTION
Simon & Schuster Inc.
Rockefeller Center
1230 Avenue of the Americas
New York, NY 10020

First Scribner Paperback Fiction edition 1998
SCRIBNER PAPERBACK FICTION and design are trademarks of Simon & Schuster Inc.

DESIGNED BY ERIKA LOPEZ

Manufactured in the United States of America

1   3   5   7   9   10   8   6   4   2

The Library of Congress has cataloged the Simon & Schuster Editions edition as follows:
Lopez, Erika
Flaming iguanas: an illustrated all-girl road novel thing / Erika Lopez
p.   cm.
I. Title
PS3562.0672F58   1997   97-3125   CIP
813'.54---dc21

ISBN 0-684-83722-6
0-684-85368-x (pbk)

This book is dedicated to my mom and my sister, both of whom may wish to remain sort of anonymous for once.

Flamingos Iguanas

★

"*Live in fame or go down in flames!*"

——a boisterous fifth-beer WWII saying

★

"I'm comin' home on a wing and a prayer."

—a very sober WWII saying

BEFORE

Magdalena and I are gonna cross America on two motorcycles. We're
gonna be so fucking cool, mirrors and windows will break when we pass by.
We'll have our own hardcore theme music that makes us throw our heads back
and bite the sky, and women wearing pink foam curlers in passing RVs will
desire us and we'll slowly turn to them at seventy-five miles an hour and
mouth "hello" back. Bugs may stick to my burgundy lipstick, but I'll just spit
them back and they'll look all the prettier for it.

Yeah / cooool. Two party bags of drugstore ice on motorcycles. The sun
wouldn't dare melt us because it would be a big, huge, major mistake.

We're gonna ride from armpit to armpit across the chest of America, joyride
full-throttle down the crack of Tennessee's ass. Bite a Grand Teton and

goose Amarillo, Texas.

Bypass Florida altogether because you get old there like <u>real</u> fast.

Sloppy-kiss the greasy lips of Louisiana.

Caress the cool, clean underside of a butcherblock from a slaughterhouse
somewhere in Montana.

Hey, there are a zillion ways to say you're going cross-country and Hallmark has a card just for you.

We'll be riding the cheapest motorcycles we can find / stopping every forty-five minutes for gas. Truck stop waitresses will wink and jam dollar bills in our happy little beautifully tanned fists, but we'll whisper "no thanks," because we don't need it / we'll live off the fumes from our estrogen.

And we'll be spitting out mango pits like fucking bullets if anyone says anything about our huge Latin American breasts.

Washington
Montana
North Dakota
Oregon
Idaho
Wyoming
South Dakota
California
Nevada
Nebraska
Utah
Colorado
Kansas
Arizona
New Mexico
Texas

New Hampshire
Maine
Vermont
Massachusetts
Wisconsin
Michigan
New York
Rhode Island
Connecticut
Iowa
Pennsylvania
New Jersey
Ohio
Illinois
Indiana
Delaware
West Virginia
Maryland
Virginia
Missouri
Kentucky
North Carolina
Tennessee
South Carolina
Arkansas
Mississippi
Alabama
Georgia
Louisiana
Florida

Chapter One
How I Met Magdalena Perez

I met Magdalena a few months ago when I accidentally ran over her cat in front of my apartment. I wanted to learn how to ride a motorcycle, so my biker friend Kelly and I rented a Vespa scooter. Kelly had a motorcycle, but it was brand new and she didn't want me banging it up.

So there I was after an hour of riding around the block, zipping around the corner at twenty miles an hour while thinking how I was gonna be a biker chick, the coolest pit tootsie in the world, looking at how good my silver rings looked on my right hand. . . the hand that controlled the throttle. . . so I ended up going a little too fast / and the faster I went the more I panicked.

It wasn't some sort of cocky, big gaping vagina thing to speed on a Vespa in front of my neighbors, no—it was more like a vicious panic-throttle-faster circle. And what came first?—panic or the egg? I didn't know, but then there was a cat darting out from underneath a 1972 Impala on blocks right next to me, and bam went the cat on my big green rental sign under the headlight. *$49.95 A DAY/10 BUCKS AN HOUR. U-SCOOT RENTALS* and a little bit o' blood-red on green is just like Christmas. Just like Christmas with the family.

But I hadn't been worried about running over neighborhood children or people's pets, because I didn't know you could run over anything on a Vespa. / I thought things like cats and children ran over you.

chapter TWO
Samba Dancing with DEATH and no Health Insurance

This was my very personal introduction to the crushing power of scooters, and therefore toasters and Epiladies.

I dropped the Vespa on the side of the road and ran back to the cat. The little cat lay in the middle of the street with its head in an Afro of blood. Kelly ran over and we both just stood there waiting, waiting, and waiting again for the cat to move. I don't know how long we stood there that way, it could've been seconds/hours/seconds. All that time a Self-Flagellating slide show was running in my head: historical sepia pictures of me as stupid/heartless/Nazi kitty-cat murderer.

I wanted to walk away in denial, go watch the news, and think the cat was faking the whole thing for attention.

Neither one of us noticed the wrinkled orange Toyota behind us until it started honking. We kept motioning for it to go around but the girl inside pointed to the empty parking space beside us with the longest rhinestone fingernail in the world. My slide show clicked off, and I angrily waved her around.

She shifted into gear and her face got small and pointy like she was gonna get that parking space whether or not we moved, and she looked down to see what we were standing over first.

"A dead cat?" The wrinkled Toyota girl yelled. "Well, move the damn thing!"

I looked back up at her with religious disgust, and, in slow motion, I saw her do a classic double take: Her eyelids peeled so far off her eyes, there was nowhere else for them to go, the corners of her purple lips stretched across her face like banana slugs and slid down as if they were passing out. Then she got whiter than cheap supermarket flour and her face spread out like a brand-new pancake.

I realized it was _her_ dead cat when she put her fists on the side of her head and started screaming. The black ponytail on top of her head covered her hands and face like a giant pom-pom sadly rooting for the Panthers.

When she finally opened her car door to get out and look at her cat, she didn't set the emergency brake, so the car started rolling toward the cat and we yelled for her to pull the brake so the cat wouldn't get run over again.

And when she finally asked us how it happened, I felt my face flush hot-wine-red and I opened my mouth to say something, but Kelly cut in and said, "Uhm," looked down, ran her fingers through her henna pageboy, and said, "Uh. . . don't know. We just got here. . . must've been a hit-and-run." Kelly looked back up at her, then at me, her eyes big and brown with concern. The woman put her face in her hands and started sobbing.

The woman was wearing a black sweatshirt with the name *Magdalena* written in glittery turquoise script, so I thought it was safe to rub her arm and say, "Uh, Magdalena, right?" She nodded. "Well, Magdalena, he looks like he went fast. And when you get hit by a car, you don't feel a thing."

I may not have been an actual run-over cat, but I did speak from experience because I got hit by a car once. I shattered my leg and even hit the windshield and everything. I woke up really sleepy on the pavement with a couple of policemen and people I didn't know in navy blue nylon jackets, looking down at me, and I smiled to myself, thinking, "Hey, wow. I'm finally the center of everyone's attention."

Kelly uncrumpled a cardboard box from the gutter and started to push the cat inside. I said wait. I wanted to feel for a pulse in case we'd have to go to the SPCA and have them give it a mercy-death shot. Ever since the scene in the movie *Casino* where Joe Pesci's brother gets beaten with a baseball bat until he's a rag doll to be buried alive, the thought of accidentally burying anything alive fucking *whips* shivers up my back like a nasty little janitor.

I gently slid my hand under the kitty cat's chin. . . waited. . . and a little flea crawled out of the fur and onto my hand because welfare as it knew it was over.

In a permanent whisper voice, the guy at the SPCA put his hand on Magdalena's shoulder, told her sorry, the cat was dead, and that he thought it was maybe 15 bucks for them to cremate the cat, $40 or $50 if she wanted her own cat's ashes back. She started sobbing into a tissue again, so I whispered for her to go outside and sit on the steps/ I'd take care of it.

I emptied my pockets on the stainless steel pet counter. They didn't have crinkly white tissue paper like humans do, so we won't swap butt cooties when we sit down for an exam. I only came up with $9 and some change. In a whisper, I begged the doctor to go ahead take all I had and cremate the cat, but to give us any ashes just as some sort of symbol-thing anyway. Like, I said I figured what difference does it make if it's cigarette ashes, incense ashes, or cat ashes? What you loved is gone no matter what you've got in your hands.

As the doctor looked at me, his eyes narrowed, his lips got thinner, his brow furrowed, and I could almost hear his sphincter tighten like a Protestant's. Then he cleared his throat, scooped up the money from the stainless steel counter, and turned, his white doctor coat flying out behind him and was gone. . . already somewhere new whispering euphemistic vet-things to someone else like creepy pillow talk.

If he weren't a vet-guy I would've thrown the box of latex gloves at his back for not answering me, but I guess I deserved it. However, you can only go through so much guilt before you're backed so far into the corner you come out like a boxing kangaroo. Never made much sense to me before, but I got it then.

"Everything's fine," I said as I sat down next to Magdalena on the stairs outside and put my arm around her/she felt like a slightly padded chair and that was okay.

That night I went home to cry and hold my own calico kitty. Like a loving mother in front of the vanity with her little girl, I tenderly picked fleas from her hair. And even though you would've thought I'd had enough killing for one day. I crushed the ones I found between my fingernails and wiped them off on the edge of a Martha Stewart magazine in the trash can.

The little dead cat reminded me how. *bam!*—just like that—you're yanked out of the game. I've spent a lot of fuckin' money on self-help and spiritual books to remind me to just cut the shit out and enjoy myself, but I always get bored or resentful after the third or fourth paragraph. Like why am I paying them to sit at home, turn the heat on full blast, stare at the ceiling, and tell me basic shit I already know?

Like creative Jell-O salads, you can only say the carpe diem thing so many ways after a couple thousand years, and simply reading about inner peace and the perfect zone diet will not make it so.

And here, this dead cat reminds me of all this carpe diem stuff for free.

I didn't see Magdalena again until a week later when I took a small cobalt glass bottle of fireplace ashes up to her place. I didn't feel guilty about the endless lying because I figured I'd never see her again, even though she lived right across the street. City Living. But instead she cringed, pushed the bottle back into my chest with both hands, looked away, and said, "No no. Not yet." It sounded like No, no, Nanette.

"Okay," I said and apologized and put the bottle into my pocket. I gave her a flash of a hug and turned on my heel to quickly say "bye" and go, but she immediately invited me in for supper, and pulled me by my arm.

I felt guilty, so I didn't pretend I had to be at an Alcoholics Anonymous meeting or something. I wasn't an alcoholic yet, but figured I would be if I keep killing animals for no good reason. I mean it's not like I'm in Alaska frying calico cat livers in onions, making Siamese earmuffs, or Persian leg warmers. Road kill for no reason is obscene.

Plastic ivy covered both sides of the narrow hallway, and she had hung up a small homemade velvet painting of her cat, bordered with gold-painted macaroni and a few pink silk flowers tucked behind the frame. We passed through three rows of beaded curtains to get to the living room: She said she wanted it to feel like you were passing through a spiritual jungle, but I felt more like a dust particle passing through a long filter.

She said sit, so I sat on her gold velour sofa and she went into the old Victorian kitchen with high ceilings. VH1 was playing music videos from the eighties on TV and I wasn't sure whether her taste in furniture was hip kitsch, or her real taste. I tried to keep a conversation going, telling her how sad it all was and asked how she was doing. I thought I caught the faint whiff of a fading, used cat box.

"You know, my cat was my best friend," Magdalena hollered back from the kitchen. I looked down and noticed a dried-up hairball on the yellow rug in front of the TV set. "Now I've got nobody. Nobody. . . no one. . ." her voice got a little higher and trailed off. I knew she was crying so I concentrated on the lampshade fringe next to me.

Now she was alone and it was all my fault. I heard some pans knocking around and echoing in the kitchen and asked her if she needed any help. I thought maybe I should offer to repair the cigarette burn in the seat of the gold velour sofa. Something. She called back and said she was fine, but thanks.

We had rice and beans, and it was so good I felt even more guilty for being an accidental shmuck. And I just kept getting worse.

So out of guilt I said yes when she asked me over for pork chops the next night and fried fish the night after that. I was pretty much a vegetarian and I hated fish with all my heart, so I figured my stabbing digestion problems all night long from the pork and the involuntary retching spasms I had to fight off with the fish were only a small part of my punishment for killing her cat and putting fireplace ashes in a cobalt glass bottle labeled "Mister Whiskers."

And later I found out that wasn't even her cat's name. I didn't know what her cat's name was, but I thought that's what it should've been, and whatever I put down would be close enough.

Turns out her cat was a woman named Snowball.

A few months after The Incident, I was over at her house watering plants, and I asked her if she wanted me to scrape the dried-up hairball off the rug and she came running in from the kitchen. "No, no, Nanette!" So I kept the bottle of ashes in my jacket pocket until the day she'd stop saying the name of that play.

Chapter Four
The Gang

It was quite a while before I felt right taking scooter lessons from Kelly again. I had to do a few therapy sessions around my murder issues, and it wasn't until the therapist convinced me the cat didn't blame me—after all, it *knew* it was darting out into a road—and, in fact, the cat wanted me to go on with my life.

When I did, Magdalena came outside from her apartment and said she wanted to learn to ride a Vespa, too. So Kelly taught us both, and one night while I was doing the dishes at Magdalena's house, I just blurted out:

"Hey, Mag! Let's start a motorcycle gang and go cross-country."

Magdalena was sitting at the chrome and pale yellow Formica kitchen table, pulling the rubber band out of her ponytail. "Just the two of us?" she asked. "We can't be a gang of two Puerto Rican girls on Vespas. Can you imagine what Girl Scouts would do to us?"

"No, no, no! We'll get real bikes," I assured her. Even though she had a velvet matador painting above her bed, she worried about how she looked to other people.

I didn't really want to be in a gang with her, but there she was, and my best friend Shannon McGillicutty wasn't my best friend anymore, ever since she'd answered that personal ad about the bread-baking guy who drove a big candy-apple pickup truck, and was so lonely that he bought a dog so he could start conversations in the park about dog shit and flea-control systems.

"Yeah, the two of us could be a gang," I answered. "It doesn't take a village, you know. I've always wanted to be in a gang called *Flaming Iguanas* in honor of our flamboyant little South American iguana brothers and sisters who are penned in like tiny lizard cows, but want to run free. All because the locals think they taste like chicken and take up less space."

"Iguanas don't *run*, Tomato."

"That's my point. Since they can't, we will run *for* them. Feel the fire of death and time nipping at our butts, making us run, live, and have no regrets. I bet you cows and iguana food-prisoners have many regrets. We'll be THE FLAMING IGUANAS!" I must've thrown my hat up in the air because it was all of a sudden across the room on top of a lamp shade. . . a little tendril of smoke got darker and ran up to the sky. Sky/Victorian ceiling—very much the same thing.

She shook her head just a little too much so her hair was flying all over the place like a pinwheel. She leafed her bottom lip like she was looking for a file and said, "I think you really need to get over your iguana thing. You've got an iguana toilet seat, iguana wallpaper, iguana oven mitts, and even that green spiky hat you always wear looks like an iguana. It's time to move on. . . why don't you have a real iguana?" Magdalena crossed her legs and looped her hands over her knees.

I gasped. "No way! They should be free!"

"So, well. . . how about. . . well, hmm. . . how about we wear pink biker jackets and call ourselves *The Snowballs?*"

I turned back around to the last few forks in the sink and pushed the soapy terry-cloth nubs between the tines. "Welllll." I started slowly and deliberately, like walking through thick snow: "We could each have our own gang and be together." I rinsed the forks, put them in the dish drainer, and turned around. "Like we could be two gangs of independent people and each have our own gang name so we don't squelch each other's identity." To my surprise I made a lot of profound sense. This was about life. A whole new carpe diem in yet another way / yet another way of tilting Jell-O salad in the fridge.

She said, "Yeah, sure. . . a gang of one. . . why not." She shrugged. She said she needed a change. Magdalena held her hairbrush in her lap with both hands and bounced it up and down. "We should go at the end of next month."

And I said okay, great.

So there, it was set. I dried my hands on the raggedy dish towel looped around the handle of the silverware drawer and walked over to her chair. She handed me the brush and slid around so her back was to me, and I started to brush her hair a hundred strokes.

I was thinking that maybe I didn't really like her that much and that I should've probably kept my mouth shut, but the truth is, by the time I was on the other side of her head I was thinking that I was way too chicken to go on my own anyhow. A gang of one can be lonely when you're threatening to kick Mount Rushmore's ass. We'd go together and save each other from a world that seemed full of the kind of serial killers they make compassionate TV movies about.

Chapter Five
Not Really a Tangent

Getting someone else to do something with you makes things somehow more real/legitimate. This is especially true for masturbation. You don't brag about how much sex you're having by yourself and how frisky you get with yourself once you get your period. No. You keep it to yourself as if somehow it doesn't really matter because you were alone.

So going with Magdalena made this trip more real and I couldn't back out now that she was in on it.

And then I thought of more reasons I should go. I thought about going to San Francisco to see my dad, whom I hadn't seen in thirteen years. The last time I'd seen my previously uptight and rigid father was when he'd driven down to New Jersey from Massachusetts to see me as the black maid in a high-school play, and afterward said he was moving to California. Just like that/didn't know why. Soon after, he started a sex toy business called Sex Toy with a woman named Hodie.

Then I found out he was a little sick. Even though he was a big-boned man, almost six feet tall, his liver was the size of a raisin and it refused to grow back anymore, and he also had brain cancer. According to Hodie, who was also his best friend, he recently started doing things like faxing slumlords 3,000 miles away in his old Harlem neighborhood looking for a job as a super. But he would've gotten more attention if he'd just hurled the fax machine in front of speeding cars on the freeway, because no one was calling him back.

But that wasn't a heavy-duty-enough reason to make me go. He wasn't like a "daddy" or anything. He just happened to be my father and I still knew where he was, so I felt some sort of responsibility to him because that's what everyone says you should have to your biological parents.

I was still afraid I was going to chicken out and cancel the next morning, and the next morning I was right, so I quickly told everyone I ran into throughout the day about my trip. The mailman and the grocery store clerks really didn't give a shit, but the gynecologist in the phone book was pretty supportive. I wanted their enthusiasm for my trip to rub off on me like childhood snot.

Random car owners who didn't even know me put their arms around me and wished me luck and told all the motorcycle accident stories they knew. Then they told me about the ones they'd seen in movies, then started making some up. "... and I heard he hasn't been the same ever since he hit that truck head-on. He holds his eyes in his head with Scotch tape and he pushes himself around in a shopping cart because he can't afford no wheelchair. . ." I'd nod, smile politely, thank them, and back away so slowly they'd say: "Hey, you losin' weight, or jest gettin' shorter?—Anyways, as I was sayin', then there was this other guy who lost half his. . ." Sometimes I think they kept going on and on, not noticing I was getting so small they could crush me between their fingers.

I tried to figure out how I could discreetly jump down a flight of stairs and break my legs so I wouldn't have to go.

chapter Six
It's a THIN Line Between Clever and Stupid

What was so wrong with watching TV? Why was I doing this? What was I proving? What the fuck was this myth that said you have to leave your job, your life, your tear-stained woman waving good-bye with a kitchen towel behind the screen door so you can ride all over the country with a sore ass, battling crosswinds, rain, arrogant Volvos, and minivans?

This is stupid. Very, very stupid. I don't even have a tear-stained dog to wave bye to me. But I told everyone I was gonna do this, so I gotta do it. . . or I will be living a life of feminist-sounding somedays. And I will be more responsible, powerful, and amazing afterward. I will be able to do anything and not self-consciously stare at elevator numbers when the doors close. I will look the other person right in the eye and nod hello.

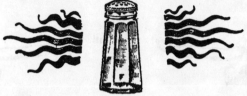

Ever since I was a kid, I'd tried to live vicariously through the hocker-in-the-wind adventures of Kerouac, Hunter Thompson, and Henry Miller. But I could never finish any of the books. Maybe because I just couldn't identify with the fact that they were guys who had women around to make the coffee and wash the skid marks out of their shorts while they complained, called themselves angry young men, and screwed each other with their existential penises.

Erica Jong was there for me in my mother's bookshelf between *Vaginal Politics* and *The Second Sex*, unapologetically running around the world in heat with her panties stretched taut around her ankles. But I never identified with her being tied to relationships like a dog to a tree / like a tongue to its mouth.

The high theater of romantic loves burns just too fucking much oil for my reality, and I spend my time trying to elevate myself above romance's trappings of jealousy, possessiveness, insecurity, and regressing to an amoebalike state.

Bullshit.

I'd love to have the kind of relationship that's immediately like being together five years, making supper and watching TV on the sofa under a cozy blanket.

I / I am a girl who feels too American for love. . . they say I'm a child of an AT&T café olé telephone-commercial future where your nose is not flat enough to offend/and not pointy enough to cut the glass ceiling.

Future child, that's me. *Hello.* It's nice to meet you.

I don't feel white, gay, bisexual, black, or like a brokenhearted Puerto Rican in *West Side Story*, but sometimes I feel like all of them. Sometimes I feel so white I want to speak in twang and belong to the KKK, experience the brotherhood and simplicity of opinions. /

Sometimes I want to feel so heterosexual, hit the headboard to the point of concussion, and have my crotch smell like bad sperm the morning after. I want the kid, the folding stroller. Please, let me stand forever in a line with my expensive offspring at Disney World. /

Sometimes I want to be so black, my hair in skinny long braids, that black guys nod and say "hey, sister" when they pass me by in the street. / I want the story, the rhythm, the myths that come with the color.

Sometimes I want to live with my hand inside of a woman so I can hear her heart beat, wake up with her smell all over me in the morning, and still feel as clean as I did the morning before/I want her to talk about her childhood until I go insane from pretending I didn't stop listening four hours ago.

Other times I wish I was born speaking Spanish so I could sound like I look without curly-hair apologies.

But I try all that and I quit it, and I try again. Really, I want to get this individualistic-thing down. I want to walk across the football field alone without looking like the last one picked to play soccer. I never was a cheerleader. I was a slut on my own with the thinking that if a tree has a good time and no one's around to hear it, it's not a slut. But sometimes you do need another tree around to double-dare you, or else you might end up doing nothing but watching TV when no one's around.

Chapter Eight
"Ma'am" is a Big Old Thing with a Republican Hairdo and Her Tits STRAPPED BACK

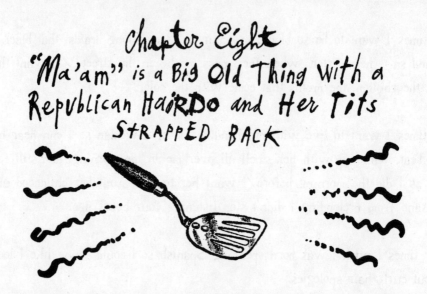

I can't say that I was friends with Magdalena solely out of guilt. Sometimes you get such a strong vibe from someone, you grab each other by the neck and become good friends. Other times you're just sitting around and someone grabs you by the neck and you're polite. So then before you know it, you're friends.

That's how it was with Magdalena. She just happened to come in my life after I lost my best friend Shannon to the boring personal-ad guy. First one she'd ever answered. Fate or desperation? Well, I tend to think just about everything in life is a combination of both. And I told Shannon to answer the ad. Hell, I even wrote the letter.

Ha ha ha.

I'd just wanted to help her out. She was tired of running into guys from South Philly with names like Franky Baroni and Tony Cristelli, who only wanted to fuck her from behind. It started giving her the creeps after a while.

So spending time with Magdalena was filling in for the loss of my friend Shannon. Shannon was my best friend, the kind of person you fall in love with creativity-wise/as long as you don't get confused and fuck things up by doing something like actually sleeping with each other.

We'd met a few years earlier in art school when Shannon started leaving little fan notes next to my work in my open studio. We became fast friends because nothing inspires fascination and loyalty like fascination and loyalty coming right at you.

We stayed up working in the studios all night. She worked on huge wooden structures that usually hung from the ceiling, and I did artsy-fartsy cartoons with old Xeroxed photos and paint because I couldn't get away with actual line-drawing cartoons in a classical art school.

We'd drink too much coffee and get incredibly jittery. By four or five in the morning our hands were bouncing around like crickets, and we'd pass out wherever we were. We never looked very attractive the next day waking up under fluorescent lights as students walked in for classes, but I never felt more alive. I felt beautiful and powerful with hair squashed on the side of my head, smelly armpits, a dissolving set of teeth, and dried-up drool running along my cheek.

31

My tits never felt perkier because these were the passion marks / the hickies of creativity and I was proud.

We'd take a whore's bath in a bathroom sink, touch up the rough spots with patchouli, and keep right on going to a new day.

It's a different kind of love. It's not like domestic-bliss love. Something else is what it is / like wanting to hang out and laugh and you think they're so fucking great you can't believe it. It can be confusing because there's definitely a sexual undercurrent, but you don't want to live or go grocery shopping with them. You want to make things/talk about loud, important things with them. And stomping down the street together, you feel like two warriors, laughing with grotesque abandon. And I think by nature it's not a jealous love, because the more the merrier, and the louder you laugh. Sore throats in the morning say how much fun you had the night before. Yeah, sort of like the sore-pussy thing.

But sometimes sore throats and pussies just mean you vomited too much the night before or you have a sexually transmitted disease.

I wonder if straight guys in Yonkers have that same frantic sexual vibe with each other after a fun night at the bar:

five guys in navy blue nylon New York Yankees jackets. . .

walking down the summer-wet streets of New York. . .

and their one night a week is over until next time. . .

time to go home. . .

oh, how long away. . .

another week of work, watching out you don't piss off the wife. . .

who cares. . .

it's dark, warm, moist.

good game tonight. . .   Yankees won 5–3. . .

gee. . . I'd really like to suck Fred's dick. . .

34

Shannon's the only one I know who's ever had the guts to say out loud, "When you meet a new good friend, it's hard to tell the difference between falling in love and wanting to fuck them or just becoming really good friends."

So far I've been able to tell the difference between who I want to fuck and who's my buddy. I never wanted to laugh and make cool things with those I wanted to fuck, because all I wanted to do was fuck, and the desire to fuck them usually only lasted three weeks. I never wanted my lovers to have anything to do with my creative friendships. That was my poker with the guys on Thursday nights.

Maybe people naturally like to keep parts of their lives sacred from their lovers, and I think that's good. Because no matter what anyone says, you can never totally be yourself with your lover. There's always some degree of "Hi, honey. Are you okay, honey? Honey, what's wrong? Oh, honey, I love you. Honey, uh, what are you thinking?" going on.

Men have gotten shit for "going out with the guys" for years, but it can't be so unnatural if so many people need to do it. Lovers may want to be woven into every fiber of a lover's life—I do, and so do other people—but you've

35

really gotta let dogs run around on their own without leashes so they can do what they want and sniff each other's butts like fine cigars once in a while. If you don't, it's bad. Very bad. All sorts of butterfly-setting-free, holding-grains-of-sand-too-tight clichés start swirling overhead like a giant Claes Oldenburg mobile.

Anyway, Shannon was out living a dime store heterosexual life after spending a few groundbreaking years pounding her fist on the table and demanding respect for being a single woman and an artist. No one listened to her, and setting an example proved too exhausting and scary, so she said fine. I'll answer a personal ad. Plus you get lots of free stuff for getting married. So Shannon threw her huge wooden sculptures in the dumpster and moved out of her loft to have a simpler life with a personal-ad guy.

Now she's a few months pregnant and they live in his house. He's so paranoid someone will steal his newsprint fantasy come true, all of his windows are set up so they don't open more than four inches, even the ones on the third floor. This broke my heart, because she became a Stepford wife with a little edge. Where did she go, my little McGillicutty girl?

At the time I met Shannon in art school, I was paying a hundred bucks to live in someone's basement on Lombard Street, a block away from abandoned buildings on South Street, and it wasn't even near any good post offices. It was closer to the post office on the bad side of town where they didn't give a shit about leaving oversized packages outside your door on the street, or not delivering that day's mail because it was already time to go home and they'd get to you tomorrow. Maybe. When you'd complain, they'd blow a big bubble with their chewing gum and raise their eyelids halfway.

My mom had come over to my basement to give me some housewarming presents, and throughout the visit she was polite, kept her lips real tight, but when she left, she walked back to her car and broke into tears.

There were no windows in my basement, only a naked lightbulb hanging behind the water heater; the floor was dirt and the walls were limestone or something, so cruddy tears ran down to the floor. The walls were rough and uneven like a cave, and a previous tenant had painted white-outline pictures of cavemen fucking bison.

The bathroom was two floors up, and whenever I was too drunk to make it upstairs for a long series of beer pees, I used the basement sink. I tried to love this romantic/pathetic existence like a slumming middle-class artist, but even Walter Cronkite would've preferred the bathroom floor at any bus station. If it'd really hit me how pathetic it was that I'd also gone to college/gotten myself $30,000 in debt/was now nearer to thirty than twenty, I would've had the decency to go inside someone's car and start crying too.

Once I tried to slit my neck open by rubbing it back and forth over the edge of the sink, but my back got tired before I could even cause a rash.

Shannon read academic theory on the toilet, and used words like *didactic* at art openings.

She lived in a peeling artist's loft on Thirteenth Street, luckily right across the street from a post office, and right above a bar called The Flaming Parrot. Her block was a hangout for black drag queens and those white hustler boys who say they're not gay if they get paid.

It was kind of creepy walking to her house and seeing a gray-haired guy in a business suit wheeling his maroon Ford Taurus to the curb to drop off a teenage guy with missing teeth, $50 richer. The kid had that no-muscle-tone frog-belly skin. He was thin, but his butt jiggled too much when he jogged across the street. The old man sped back over the bridge to the Jersey suburbs with a MY CHILD'S AN HONOR STUDENT AT CHERRY HILL HIGH SCHOOL sticker on his car's bumper.

The drag queens were great and they could throw their voices like New York Yankee home runs. They kept their plastic fingernails on until 2 A.M. when the bars let out / then you'd hear laughing, slaps, and shrieking in the streets. Some fights got serious, and then they'd growl, stroke their adam's apples so they'd grow big and hard, peel their plastic nails off, and punch each other in the alleys.

In the morning there were enough colored fingernails on the sidewalks to make it look like New Year's Day.

Shannon was little, but she was pretty strong. She could carry one of those old white refrigerators up three flights of stairs, argue with a neighbor about some article in *The Smithsonian* on the way, and still have enough strength to flirt with a guy by castrating him.

She was about five feet two and she had the kind of small face that you expected to see on the cover of *Classic Irish Songs* in a secondhand record store. She wore her red hair in a bob, with one side neatly folded behind an ear like a curtain in New Jersey. Her eyes were small and bright blue, and I don't remember her taking the time to blink that much/she had an intense squint, even at rest. Sometimes she'd do a little Irish jig she learned from her dad, and go "diddle lee dee" until we both nearly peed ourselves.

She'd had sex with an art chick once. They used to be roommates and she'd go down on Shannon but she wouldn't let Shannon touch *her*. She got off by making Shannon sit on the edge of the bed and look away while she masturbated looking at color-Xerox pictures of guys fucking each other. Shannon got to thinking sex with girls was dumb and she asked That Girl to move out once we started hanging out.

That Girl got real depressed and started leaving leftover fried eggs and bacon under her bed to rot along with a lot of used tea bags. Then in a last-ditch effort to get Shannon to run back into her vegetarian arms, she threw out all the chicken in the freezer, bought the *Moosewood Cookbook*, and started making huge pots of lentil soup in a food-equals-love campaign.

Finally, in a low-cut black dress from a thrift shop, she stormed out after checking around for the last of her things.

Men seemed to irritate Shannon even though she was always looking for one. She couldn't understand why when she'd finally go on a date, there was never a second one. When they'd come by to pick her up, she'd greet them with her voice high up in her forehead. But as the night wore on, she'd discuss sexual politics in a voice that closed slowly like a fist and smash their opinions against the walls like eggs.

After dessert, she'd undo a button on her blouse and make her eyes soft, bring her voice back up to the top of her forehead, and slowly reach for her date's hand. When she felt the sweat on his palms evaporate, the trap was set:

"And what do *you* think of what Woody Allen and O. J. Simpson have done to women?"

Now I don't think anyone should use those two guys' names in the same sentence. I may not know what I'm talking about when it comes to tedious details, but I've known a lot of white girls who get giddy around big black men and then they have these loud and crazy relationships complicated with bouts of historical low self-esteem and racism strapped together with No-Nonsense-Pantyhose sex.

It pisses everyone off and bossy white men and single black women want them to learn a lesson, because there's only like one black man for fifty black women, but it's best to stay out of fetish relationships of any kind. Don't mess with other peoples' fetishes.

And Woody Allen/he can fuck whoever wants to fuck him back. We shouldn't be able to say a whole lot about it no matter how weird because we've got our own creepy surprise parties. And in the old days, before our chairs had so much goddamned padding, this kind of stuff was considered normal.

Well, whatever Shannon's dates answered to her O. J. and Woody question, it wasn't feminist enough, and later they'd wish they'd chewed their legs off and crawled out of the restaurant fast/but their mistake was that they never wanted to make a scene.

And by the time she was done with them, they were propped up against Calvin Klein underwear posters at the bus stop, drooling, with a bloody stump between their legs.

She didn't really even know what she was doing. She always cried afterward and wondered whether they'd call her again. When it came to men, she reminded me of a pit bull in a Walt Disney movie—all the while it was in the ring fighting to the death with another dog's jugular vein between its teeth, it really just wanted to cuddle in front of the fire and sing happy songs.

Really, she was a hundred pounds and cute when she wasn't saying anything.

But I understand. I guess it was inevitable she'd dump the loneliness, rejection, and hard work for familial happiness. The life of a woman artist isn't exactly what anyone in her right mind would choose if anyone told you the truth of it on career day. Firefighter with a wife at home fixing supper always beats everything else hands down.

To be a budding girl artist with a clue is to be cynical and bitter even before you hit thirty. And Shannon wanted magic back. She wanted to be moved by a statue of the Virgin Mary crying and not look in back for the spigot. Cynicism is a boring and dull old man's disease people have no business getting when they're young.

It makes for trendy, cranky, stand-up humor, but I'm gonna believe in Ralph Nader and Bob Ross of the TV show *Joy of Painting*. I don't care what anyone says. I've got to believe, because it's gotten to the point where I sob for hope and joy whenever I hear a Good Samaritan story on the news.

Do you know who Bob Ross was? He would do an entire country scene in twenty-five minutes, and the whole time his calm voice was talking about "happy phthalo green" and "happy little water lines" and giving me paintbrush chills all over my skin, to the tips of my fingers.

And when he whispered, " . . . Let the brush shake and tremble just a little bit," it was absolute art porn for me. / Bravo, Bob.

CHAPTER NINE
Yeah

And here I was with my new friend's Puerto Rican hand around my neck in friendship. I wanted to have my hand around her neck, too. Have it be mutual. I knew that if that urge to grab didn't come right away for me, it would never come.

chapter Ten
FLAM

I went out and got myself a used motorcycle jacket and started to embroider the name of my gang on the back. That was before I found out you're supposed to embroider on something soft first, and then sew the edge of the patch on the jacket.

So I didn't know all that, and I only got the letters F-L-A-M on my jacket before I got something like carpal tunnel syndrome and the skin on the tips of my fingers was like ground beef. Have you ever tried to push a needle and thread through leather a thousand times?

I didn't care about the FLAM thing. Once I put on the jacket, I was leader of the pack, armed with a Jell-O theory of independent togetherness.

I felt so cool. I walked across the street to Magdalena's apartment and asked her her bra size. She said C-cup, so I daringly pinched the alpha dog's cheek and said, "Okay baby, that's what I'm gonna call you from now on."

"What?" She winced, pulled her face back and rubbed her cheek.

"Yep." I said, "we need some nicknames, so I'm gonna call you C-cup. I like that. C-cup. Has a nice ring to it."

"Well then, what am I supposed to call you?"

"You don't."

"Well, that's not very fair."

She was right. One thing: I was raised Quaker, so fairness is extremely important. More important than what you're not supposed to do. So I told her why: "Tomato's already my nickname. My real name's Jolene. Like in Dolly Parton's song."

Magdalena squished her nose up in disgust. "I don't know any Dolly Parton songs."

"Too fuckin' bad, babe." I was really getting into this. . . challenging Magdalena's previous alpha female position. My guilt was fading away like a long-time headache, and now we were like wild dogs fighting for social position.

"Whatever."

Satisfied, I loosened my canine jaws from the side of her face. She was down on the ground and now we both knew who had to obediently stand still while her ass was being sniffed. "Okay," I said. "I'm going over to my mom's house since this is the last weekend before we go. I've gotta say good-bye and stuff."

an uncircumcised penis

Chapter Eleven
The Medium-Length Good-bye

In my supercool FLAM motorcycle jacket, I took the speedline over the bridge to New Jersey so I could hang out with my family as if it were the last time, but the two of them wanted to watch TV.

I guess they were in denial. Yeah. Denial. I knew they loved me.

Either that, or they didn't believe that this time I really was in my own motorcycle gang of one. They'd stopped performing enthusiasm parades for me around the time I told them I was thinking of quitting art school so I could be a cartoonist and make a living being a truckdriver or a surgeon. And right there in front of them, as I was excitedly explaining how it all would work, images of damaged body parts danced in my brain and I thought about how we're all gonna die. I dropped into an existential depression that lasted three or four weeks on my mother's sofa in front of cable TV.

My family is just my mother and my sister when my mom and her girlfriend of fifteen years are split up. They seriously split up all the time and move out of each other's houses. Between them, there are like four or five houses all over South Jersey because some of them are "too painful" to move back into.

My mom's a real strong woman. She used to drive us on long trips with my sister and me in the back seat of our army green '72 Impala, seeing which one of us could sound more like Cher singing "Half-breed."

My mom, my sister, and I, we're like the Judds, and I like to fancy I'm like Wynonna. Wynonna and I are both extremely emotional and have weight problems in families of long legs and small asses. But despite that level of thin-torso resentment, my mom, my sister, and I are a very close and loving family and it's pretty hard to get a word in edgewise. We don't apologize for how we are because we think we're right.

And I'm not too sure about Wynonna's mom and sister, but my mom and my sister just naturally knew how to always be appropriate, while I never had a clue. They were always well pressed and knew not to lunge for the turkey leg at someone else's house. It's tough being born without an "appropriate" barometer. To this day I still feel like I have spinach in my teeth, the back of my skirt tucked in my underwear, and toilet paper stuck to my shoe.

I bet you 25 percent of the people labeled schizophrenics are actually people who just don't know how to be appropriate.

So I felt left out as a kid and started to imagine my childhood was a traumatic TV movie. As I walked home from grade school, I'd hear dramatic orchestral music as if I'd accomplished something heroic. By the age of eight, I was terrified that I couldn't remember every single minute of my life for future movie autobiographies, and wondered if every trip to the dentist had to be in a thorough life story.

And then I remembered hearing about some lady who had brain surgery, and when they accidentally touched a piece of her brain, she remembered many details from her childhood she'd forgotten. So I relaxed and figured if it came down to that, I could have brain surgery to remember everything.

I sat next to my sister on the sofa and started blowing in her ear. She smacked me on the leg so she could watch TV.

"Don't worry, Glena-Glane. Momma-girl knows about our special drive-in-movie kind of love," I said in a cheap southern accent.

I joke about incest with my sister and thank God it doesn't bother my mother. When I want to know if I look good in something, I ask Glena if it makes her want to have sex with me. When she doesn't say anything I like to believe it means "why, of course." I tell her if we were back in West Virginia we wouldn't have to be ashamed of our love and she could bear my children. And in case something went wrong with the kids, there are special schools, you know.

Her real name is Elena. Elena Rodriguez. And I love her so much, I want to follow her into the next life so I can hang out with her and laugh a lot.

Ever since she got a *coupon val-u pak* in the mail addressed to her as "Glena" about five years ago, Glena just stuck. I switch between calling her Glena-Glane or Elena-Glane depending on my mood. And I call my mother Momma-girl because I like to pretend we're in the South and Momma-girl is the closest thing to a name like Bobby Sue or Daisy Mae while keeping the respectful "mom" thing going.

Elena-Glane understands the bad taste that makes me who I am, and she gets all my bestiality jokes. She doesn't make me shut up unless we're in public, and even then I ignore her and know she'll still love me. Now, I tell you, that in itself is priceless. When you can smell your panties in front of someone and they keep flipping pancakes, then, hey—you don't let that person go.

Ventilated Sides

Elena's skin is a lot lighter than mine. My mom's got freckles and she has to use sunblock to like the fiftieth power. My dad's pretty dark brown. So we got mixed skin. My sister, she ended up with pretty yellow Perdue-chicken skin, and when she gets a tan, she's golden, and I call her my little *pollo*. When she looks like that, I tell her she should be on some mechanic's calendar. Then she usually calls me buttwipe and throws something at me. Guess I touched a nerve.

Me, I ended up kind of gray brown. Elena-Glane calls me island girl when I get real dark. One time I was at the Jersey shore, and I guess some people must've thought I was originally white, because of my pointy nose features and all, and they'd never even seen me before but they kept saying, "Oh, my God, did you ever get dark! Wow! Dark! How did you get so dark?" They were still pink like cartoon pigs, and I told them to cover their deck in tinfoil and lie down naked.

54

We empty the dishwasher a lot when we're at my mom's house and Elena and I scream like squealing munchkins for no reason. It scares any adults who are around, but Mom's so used to us she forgets to apologize to company. But my mom's also the kind of woman who'll tell the waiter that you can't have sugar because you have a yeast infection. At times like that, all you can do is smile and repeat to yourself under your breath:

All witnesses eventually die.
All witnesses eventually die.

I'm so glad my mother gave birth to Elena-Glane because she's like a built-in best friend.

Being only two years older, I still feel so protective of her that I can't imagine what actual parents must go through. All of a sudden, the world would be a place full of boogeymen and army recruiters grabbing at my children. / Wow. The responsibility boggles my mind, and I think I would end up some some kind of crazy bigfoot-Catholic-mother-thing.

When my cat was in heat, and jumped out of a second story window at 4 A.M. to get outside and fuck some man cat, I chased her around the backyard with a toilet brush for an hour just so she'd stay pure.

And I wish I'd had a toilet brush when Elena was seven and the judges totally forgot to taste her plate of brownies at a day camp brownie-making contest. Some snotty kid won from a mix with chocolate syrup, and he jumped up and down on his mother's leg like a Chihuahua.

My sister counted her brownies, and the same twenty were still there. She said something to a counselor, but the counselor immediately said all twenty were still there because they'd only tasted little teeny, tiny microscopic pieces. My sister knew that was a load of crap because her brownies were in perfect shape.

And being from our polite but firm family, she excused herself and quietly had a polite crying fit in the parking lot. She knew she should've won, because even then she was a perfectionist, and they were the kind of brownies they'd serve in Paris. She had to melt dark chocolate over a double boiler, fold in fluffy dairy products—and what seven year old *folds* anything, much less dairy products in a recipe?

The unfairness broke my heart, because you should've seen how happy she was making brownies with my grandmother. Glena-Glane was proud, and she marched her brownies up to that long folding table like she was Miss Universe. I wanted to threaten them with a toilet brush, but I knew they wouldn't understand because they already looked at us like we were leftovers from some liberal free-love moment in the sixties.

But it didn't ruin her life. It only made her a tougher, stronger baker, and that's what's important.

Yeah, Elena-Glane and I have a special bond and I don't give a fuck what all the therapists say about "symbiosis." I've been in therapy half my life and you know what? I found the more you're aware of anything, the worse off you are in the long run because you have to live with yourself. As far as I can tell, there are no prizes for having your shit together. At its best, you can talk about how fucked up other people are with an air of authority, and you can scare the shit out of yourself at night with the thought of growing old alone and right.

Look at dogs.

Dogs are happy even as they chase balls out of fifth-floor windows.

When I first started group therapy at thirteen, I was with a bunch of adults who came to group right after work. A lawyer, a nurse, and a wealthy coke fiend who wore leopard-print pants and shiny gold high heels. I can't remember the other people's careers. Maybe that's why they were in therapy and always regretting something. They hadn't even chosen careers worth remembering.

The day after a session, I would go back to my junior high school, hang out in the girl's room smoking long skinny cigarettes that made my hips look smaller, and say things like, "Yeah, Jenny, I hear your pain, you seem to have some conflicting feelings about sleeping with Maggie's boyfriend. Perhaps you're internalizing rage against Maggie."

My sister stayed quiet enough to avoid therapy—except for the mandatory biannual family session—and my mom's girlfriend thought that's why she went through a normal rebellious period, but I think Elena was always the little rebel because she had to grow up with a lot of condescending people who insisted they knew better as they were busy punching each other or drinking too much.

Now don't get me wrong, counseling can be great and save your life, but it can also drive you insane. Therapy people can fuck up anything, like growing up. We couldn't go out and even play at getting drunk at seventeen, and write sad folk songs about it because we actually "knew (too much) better" and my mother would've analyzed our behavior to a pulp.

With too much therapy, there are few good, unanalyzed times to be had. And therapy people will talk bad about everybody else's problems but call it "analyzing."

At twenty-six, I finally raged against the I'm-okay-you're-okay machine, and when I wanted to leave, they said I should stay or I'd become fucked up again/wouldn't be able to cope.

What? I couldn't even cope now with everyday people. I could only cope with my little paid once-a-week group, while other people were out, actually having sex, moving in with each other, laughing and fighting, denying their feelings—in essence, fucking up, making mistakes, learning, and actually living life.

So I made my way out into the world without any borrowed wisdom.

But the world was a talk show where everyone was processing too much, overanalyzing first dates, blaming everything they did on their parents, and talking bad about other people under the guise of analyzing them and therefore helping them out.

And after the big bill has been paid, I have learned only two things I know for sure:

> (1) Don't talk yourself out of doing anything except for killing people.

> (2) If you've hit thirty and are still blaming crap on your parents, you've got entirely too much time on your hands.

Weird crap's always gone on and it always will / I think it's part of human nature up there with giving tourists honest directions or killing wolves because they're in _our_ backyards. But remember. . .

> _You're_ not fucked up. It's your _behavior._

I have gone back to old-fashioned denial, avoidance, and hard-assed impatience simply because I can get things done faster. But when little white guys go around with their student loans paid off and their hands on their hips, running their fingers through well-cut hair, crying, "I! I!—I am a _very_ angry young man!" I just want to puke up all the strawberries I bought with the last of America's food stamps into their lap.

Sorry, mister *very* angry young man. If this were a gay porno movie, that janitor would put down that mop and come over here and wipe the vomit off your lap until you got a hard-on, then he'd pull your 100 percent cotton Dockers around your ankles and fuck you up the ass so hard, you'd start singing *"clang clang went the trolley!"* until your prostate gland moved to San Francisco.

I love gay porn. Especially the kind where they have the straight guy *hesitate* a few minutes before he gives the truckdriver a blow job.

While Momma-girl and Elena-Glane were watching TV, I picked up a shiny sale circular. I *love* sale circulars. They're so suburban and *affordable*. Models come alive from clip art, wear polyester pants, and sell barbecue grills for ten bucks and white plastic lawn chairs that cost less than a cheese sandwich. When a commercial came on, I looked up at my lovely family and quickly asked, "Howaboutpizzafordinner?"

While we were trying to decide what to get *on* the pizza, their show came back on and they told me to shut up, so I went out to get fried chicken instead.

Even though I was twenty-seven and my sister was twenty-five, we made Mom divvy up the chicken so we wouldn't fight over the breast. / Breasts are a running theme in our lives. / As it was, the chicken wasn't all that amazing, so we didn't fight over anything. Elena got the Cheerios out of the cabinet instead, and we fought over the prize in a halfhearted way.

I threw my body across the sofa like a movie star and started crying. This might've been the last time I'd see her and we were waving our hands in the air like we just didn't care.

Elena handed me a tissue, sat on the floor, and turned up the TV.

I remembered a bunch of years ago on some Christmas morning when we both woke up at Mom's house. I must've been home from highway-robbery art school, in my bathrobe putting the cow teakettle on, and Elena came down the stairs holding up her right hand with a horror-movie look on her face.

"What's wrong?" I mirrored her a horror-movie look back, then high-fived her hand thinking that's what she wanted me to do.

"Aaah!" She swung away from me like I was a monk on fire, and she cupped her hand to her body like it was loose or something.

"What's wrong?"

"Nothing!"

"Come on, Glane. What's wrong with your hand? Have you finally gone insane from all that 'rainbow-rainbow' wallpaper in your room?"

My mother and my sister loved to decorate in high-blood-pressure colors. Elena had a lime green shag carpet on her floor, one orange wall, one primary blue wall, and the other two had wallpaper that said "rainbow rainbow" over and over again in all the roygbiv colors (red, orange, yellow, green, blue, indigo, violet). It made me nervous, so mostly we chatted in the bathroom or my room, which was painted chocolate brown and had a deep rust-colored rug. It was like a love pad because I'd gone through some sort of Harvey's Bristol Creme jazz phase, and fantasized about bringing sweaty black basketball players home from high school.

"*Nothing's* wrong with me."

"Fine. This is why you can't be intimate. You hold all your pain inside, Elena." Low blow. Therapy teaches you how to hit below the belt, and as I said, Elena was the black sheep when it came to therapy. Even on vacation mornings at the beach, we'd all read to each other from our daily affirmation calendars before we started our day in the sun. I'd read mine with many pauses like an important speech.

"Okay. I'll tell you," Elena gave in, "but you promise you won't ever write about it in one of your cartoons one day?"

"Jeez, what do you think I am? Some heartless artist who exploits the people close to me?"

"Okay. I guess you're right. That'd be pretty cold-hearted."

"That's right. Well now, what's bothering you, little muffin cup of my life?"

She held her right hand up in front of my face and started shaking. "See that?"

"What?"

"My last three fingers are numb."

"Last fingers starting from where? Your thumb or your pinky?" I turned her hand around like a greeting card I'd finished reading.

"I think aliens kidnapped me last night and cut off my fingers, then sewed them back on before they brought me back home."

I looked at her, ready to laugh. This was imaginative. More imaginative than when she had her imaginary witch friends when she was seven and I was nine.

See, when I was nine years old, our father had come back into our lives for the first time since I was four and Elena was two, and I went to live with him. I'd hated my mom for having a female lover whose face was half crippled from polio. She had a scary laugh like a jammed engine because her vocal cords were all fucked up. I never wanted my friends to see her. It seemed to me that if my mom was gonna sleep with women, couldn't she find someone who looked like Barbie? It was 1976 in West Virginia; women who looked like Blue-eye-shadow Barbie *were* West Virginia.

So, because my mom wasn't being a Malibu Barbie lesbian, I went to live with *Dad.* I said his name like it was "*wow.*" I also liked that we were almost the same color brown, because I was starting to think I was really adopted.

Alone with my amazingly uptight dad in his tiny boring apartment, I convinced my sister to come live with me in Massachusetts so she and I'd be together. My mom was into making crazy stir-fry dinners, and Elena and I would come up with ways of throwing away the mushrooms and green peppers so we wouldn't have to eat them. Most of the time, after the dishes were all washed, Mom opened the napkin bundles in the trash and made us eat the soggy green peppers and mushrooms because she was German.

I told Elena *Dad*—(la la la)—never made green peppers or mushrooms. She'd love it there.

But this was before he had his midlife crisis/brain tumor and took off for California. He was no fun / he was rigidly silent like a Nazi general at home—except for when he was walking on campus. Then he held his head up, rested his hand on my shoulder, walked like he was surveying his grounds, smiled and nodded occasionally to an acquaintance. When he ran into a giddy grad student who wanted to get strapped down and saddled by a father figure, he acted like he was Ricardo Montalban selling her a Corinthian leather dick with a Puerto Rican accent / she'd be over for dinner at 7 P.M. and home by 8 A.M.

He'd never had kids before and he thought we were like dogs, so he bought cases of tomato soup and fed it to us every day with a glass of water. Elena hated tomato soup and she really started hating it there. She'd been duped big time and wanted her money back.

Dad got tired of having dog-kids around. He liked fucking in his rigid little love pad and we seriously cramped his style. As the head vagina in the household, I'd get jealous and put itching powder in the coed's panties the next morning while they were in the shower. I wanted my immaculately clean dad to think they had crabs and go "Ew, yuck. I'm leaving you, coed girl."

One restrained Sunday night, after *60 Minutes* was over, Elena faked her evening shower and wet the top of her curly hair. When she came into the living room to say good night, he saw all this dry hair around her head and quietly dragged her back into the bathroom and punched her out against the tile wall for faking. I felt so guilty about convincing her to move with me so she wouldn't have to eat green peppers, I didn't talk to her so much anymore.

She stayed in our room by herself and talked to her imaginary witch friends in their private witch language for the rest of the time we lived with him. When I'd run back in the room to get something, she'd watch me out of the corners of her eyes, speak to her imaginary witch friends louder so I'd feel left out. But I made fun of her instead, and went back out to play. I hated staying in that apartment because he ignored us and lit matches after he took shits so we'd never know he was human enough to smell bad.

None of us took care of Elena when she was little. She was quiet and stayed out of the way, and now we were letting aliens kidnap her, cut off her fingers so they could study them and sew them back on.

Chapter Twelve
Less Than a Week
Before We Go, and I Still
Don't Know How to Actually Ride
a Motorcycle and I Don't
Even HAVE a
Motorcycle.

WISH I'D WORN PANTIES.

Chapter Thirteen
But, Damn, I Look So Good in My Biker Jacket, I Point to myself in the mirror and Say THiNGS like, "HEY baby... YEAh, I'm TALkin' to you."

Clutch? First, second, third, and fourth? What was everyone talking about?

Many times I leaned over the railing from the third-floor landing and thought of just tossing myself over. Splat, just like that. But figured with my luck, I'd end up with some kind of horrid literary Ethan Frome lesson; end up a screaming vegetable salad, and die with old yellowing plastic dusty things in my house, instead of landing with a simple broken leg.

All those bony-nosed literary academics and critics in the sky would be creaming their pants over this kind of irony. Someone who thought she was leader of the pack—and ha!—you are now a vegetable! The proud Madame Bovary stabbed in the temple with scissors! Miss Haversham in a stinky yellow wedding dress for no apparent reason! Michael Jackson with all that money and rhythm and a skin disease! Ha!

I looked across the street, and saw I was quickly losing alpha dog status: Magdalena had gone out and gotten herself a shiny pink vinyl motorcycle jacket, and her brother had fixed up his chopper for her.

I rolled my own cigarette because it was a helluva lot cheaper, not because it looked cooler, and I thought for a minute. I thought about the Vespa and ironic Ethan Frome. And then ironic lung cancer.

I flicked the cigarette between two parked cars and went inside to eat a lot of ice cream.

CHAPTER FOURTEEN

Even Though She Vomited, I THINK She Had a good Time

Some guy gave his drug dealer a motorcycle because he couldn't come up with the cash.

Then the drug dealer put a sign for 500 bucks on the bike, and and a guy named Ivan Leibowitz saw the sign and gave him 500 bucks.

My friend Ivan got a motorcycle so he could ride around feeling the cold spots under the trees with his long-haired girlfriend. They were real sweet for each other, but Ivan learned there are no love guarantees when his girlfriend left him to try other people out. She was looking for bodice-ripping romantic high theater like Madame Bovary. She just didn't get it that when someone asks you how your day was, and actually cares about the answer, that it doesn't get much better than that.

So Ivan let his motorcycle gather cobwebs and leaves in his backyard until I took a cab over to see if he knew of any hundred-dollar bikes for sale, or if I could borrow his for a little trip cross-country.

He opened the door in a tattered red flannel bathrobe and sneakers. His normally long brown rabbi ringlets looked more like dreadlocks, and he held a bowl of Cap'n Crunch to his chest in a translucent blue Tupperware bowl. He said, here, take it and have a blast, and he jammed the keys and the pink title in my hand, shuffled backward and shut the door.

I stood out in his front yard, realizing I didn't know how to ride the motorcycle back over the bridge to my house. I had a highway to go on and everything.

So I knocked on the door and asked Ivan to teach me how to ride so I could get home.

Poor guy. He spent three hours teaching me how to shift into gear, and every time he even touched the bike to help me lift it off the ground, he broke into tears.

By the time I felt ready to go, there were a whole bunch of dead bugs in his congealed Cap'n Crunch. I felt guilty about that, but he waved me away and said don't worry about it.

I took the long way back home. A whole bunch of pothole roads with speed bumps so I could avoid the highway. We only lived seven or eight miles apart, and it only should've taken twenty minutes with traffic, but it took me quite a few hours. I won't even say how long. Just that I didn't do real well with turns or stopping without stalling, so I kept wiping out. And now I know what motorcycle jackets are really for.

I pulled up right below C-cup's window and started honking. I didn't put my feet down fast enough so I fell over. She came down, helped me pick up the bike, and asked if I would really be ready to leave tomorrow. I said sure, of course, and I started to roll a cigarette because if I lived long enough to get cancer, I'd be lucky.

Chapter Fifteen
Come on, You Never Want to Talk About How You're Going to Die

I plan on getting cancer now so I won't be surprised when I get it later. With all the crap in our food, water, and air, I think it's the new way of dying "naturally." Thoughts of getting hit by trucks and cancer inspire me to have a good time now. I'm not gonna go through the chemotherapy microwave because it'll just come back later and I'll have to go through the whole thing again of telling everyone how sick I am and saying good-bye to them.

chapter sixteen
THE BIG DAY

It turned out to be the kind of day where I would've rather been at home wearing slippers and screaming at children outside my window. Perhaps I gave myself far too much credit for summoning the strength to throw my terry-cloth slippers under the bed and walk out the door, but I didn't care. We all have our mountains.

On our way out of Philadelphia, C-cup was doing real well keeping up with the speed limit, and I think I was going as fast as 15 mph over the Commodore Barry Bridge. I don't know for sure because I don't have a working speedometer. Wimps who went into four-wheel drive over speed bumps in their Jeep Cherokees and Isuzu Troopers passed me, shaking their fists. I was terrified and embarrassed, belting out "God Bless America" to calm myself for the first hour I was on the bridge, before I realized, *shit. I'm gonna be pressured into making one dumb move into an oncoming truck, so this Isuzu clown on his car phone can get to his office a little faster? I'll crash and my life will be fucked up, while he gets back on his phone to boss people around who make more money than I ever will. All for a few minutes?—*

"Fuck you! *You* ride this goddamned thing!" was as clever as I could get with death humping me. I'd try to run them off the bridge as if I were in a movie, but at fifteen miles an hour, you can't even scratch the paint.

C-cup was waiting for me at a 7-11 on the other side, leaning against her bike and looking at her watch.

We drove for another two hours before I wanted to stop in a small rural town in Pennsylvania where there were a lot of cows and Amish people. It was drizzling, and we'd seen a billboard for a happy family campground a few miles away. I was hunched over in the fetal position, getting an ulcer because I

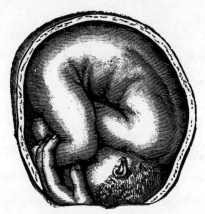

couldn't ride faster than maybe twenty-five miles an hour, so we followed the billboard's directions and pulled into a tacky theme-park campground.

We saw professional families walking from their cars in descending order of height, and we were scared. There were ten foot tall wooden statues of smiling Amish people lining the entrance and all it took was one look for us to turn around and get back on the main road. I didn't know how to do a nice little turn, so I had to go around the entire parking lot to turn around. I was a little embarrassed because up ahead, C-cup had to pull over and wait for me. She was looking at her watch again and I knew she was the alpha dog again.

No one waved flags or admired us biker chicks from the sidelines as we rode out of this little Amish town. / And thank God. The only ones who looked at us were the kids on the sidewalks when we screamed as their toys flew in front of our bikes. And the only thing I was spitting out of my chapped lips was my hair, all sticky with bug guts and a little rain.

The only theme music playing in my music-video life was the theme to *Sesame Street*. What happened to the cool, laid-back part of riding? My heart stopped every time I had to come to a complete stop or turn a corner.

Sesame Street and death. My thoughts fuck each other badly, and the muppets suffer for it: *Big Bird's too old and too fat to get out of his chair, living in some old five floor walk-up in New York. Grouchy, drinking Diet Pepsi, screaming at Maria with maggots between his rotting Big Bird toes. He was a diabetic, dontcha know? But Maria's not there. She spends her free time leaving anonymous messages on Rita Moreno's answering machine, and Oscar the Grouch is swallowing shoelaces and begging for money on a bed of nails with Robert Crumb's brother on the streets of San Francisco. In the late afternoon, they molest mannequins in Chinatown and pay for cheese burritos in dimes. . .*

We ended up driving another three hours because the next campground marked on our map was farther than we thought, so it was ten o'clock when we pulled in. But there was a big gate that was shut and locked, and a brown wooden sign in yellow letters that said, NO CAMPING. We just straddled our bikes with the engines still running, and looked at it for about fifteen minutes.

Some headlights started coming toward us in the dark, and a Camaro pulled up to the fence. A young guy got out, said "hello" and unlocked the fence.

I was too depressed to say anything, so C-cup asked, "Uh, do you know where we can camp?"

He put his hands on his hips and thought. "Hmmm. Well, you can't camp here. I work here and it's closed now."

"We just need a place to sleep."

"Well, I think there's an RV campground about thirty miles north of here."

Thirty miles? At my top speed of twenty-five miles an hour—with six or seven cigarette and bathroom breaks—it'd be morning by the time we got there. I dropped my helmet head on my handlebars and wanted to go home. Concentrating on the gaping hole where my speedometer was supposed to be, I started sending the Camaro guy telepathic suggestions. . . *Let us camp here anyway. . . let us camp here anyway. . .*

"Okay." C-cup pulled her map from under the bungee cords on her gas tank and asked him what town it was in. He answered her, and we started to back our bikes up with our feet.

Damn. Fuck. Cripes.

"Good luck," he waved.

"Thanks," we yelled back under our helmets.

C-cup's foot slipped in the gravel and her bike fell down and she jumped off.
He came over to help her pick the bike up and after it was back up, he wiped
his hands on his pants and asked, "Are you just looking for a place to camp?
Just a place to put up a tent? Because, well. . . if you are, there's a big field
in front of my house, and uh, you could just set up your tent there. . ."

I jumped on it before C-cup could even hesitate, "Yes! Yes! Yes!"

We introduced ourselves and followed his faded maroon Camaro home.
I wondered if this would turn out to be a cheap and wild sexual experience.
A man in a '78 Camaro, two chicks on bikes. Hey, I'd gone to high school in
New Jersey, and it didn't take a rocket scientist to figure we had the makings
of a Bruce Springsteen song.

I wanted my hair high and stiff, just like I wanted my Camaro boss. . .

Oh, baby, we were born to run.

I'd forgotten what it was like to sleep totally outside, and being a romantic, I wanted to fall asleep looking at the stars. No-nonsense C-cup promptly fell asleep in the tent, and I felt safe with her three feet away and our host fifty yards away in his house.

I snuggled into my cozy down sleeping bag, but the zipper wouldn't work. That was okay. I tucked both sides under me and looked up at the sky. / A huge clear sky of stars. The trees at the edges of my eyes became the size of frozen broccoli, the crickets became the heartbeat of the planet and so I started feeling sleepy like a little embryo in a down sleeping bag.

Then I realized I had to take off my glasses, but I was too tired to move. I couldn't fall asleep without breaking them—but what if I decided ahead of time not to turn over?—No. You can't make promises like that in West Virginia, so I woke up all over again to take them off and then the sky was blurry. Fine. I'd just go to sleep then.

At three in the morning I woke up freezing, wet with dew. The edges of my sleeping bag were soaked and I was totally wet. Now feeling like a very cold embryo, I walked over to the tent in the fetal position and started whining. C-cup had to wake up and move over.

Chapter Seventeen
No Matter How Beautiful You Are, Your Pee Smells Bad

Ah, the romance of ignorance. . . sometimes you only see what you want to see in someone, and it works until you leave the bar or until you learn their last name.

After a couple of days on the road with her telling me about the crap inside her belly button, bragging about how much dandruff she could scratch into her lap, and still wearing the same jeans she'd peed in the second night we camped out because she forgot that when you squat, you also have to push your pants forward, toward your knees, it was all I could do to say, *"Here, uh, you can have the tent to yourself. . . yeah, I'll just sleep on that rock over there. No, really. . . I don't even like shelter that much."*

84

I could've ignored all that very well and continued to sleep on rocks or moldy picnic tables. I could've even ignored the fact that she was the kind of girl to take a good time in a choke hold and pin it to the mat until it cried for mercy. But she wanted to ride ten miles above the speed limit on a straight superhighway and go twelve hours a day so we could get across America as quickly as possible. She had only two definite agendas: one was to at least pass by a Route-66 sign; and the other was to buy a hunting knife. Then she could go home satisfied.

Every minute had to be totally planned out with the map wedged in her waistband, and her hands on her hips like a German Girl Scout.

What had happened to the fluffy velvet Puerto Rican C-cup? Had I left her behind for this new over-achieving bitch girl in a pink jacket who didn't know how to squat and clear her pants?

I wanted to wear white cotton dresses, pick daisies in a field, sing heterosexual folk songs to every cow, and have my picture taken in front of America's post offices.

I was willing to flex on the white dress and the heterosexual folk songs, but when she got allergies from riding open-faced behind cars, and started sneezing in my face while we were sleeping in the tent without covering her mouth, that was it. I could actually smell the spit in her sneezes and the honeymoon fell off the desk like a little guinea pig, so I gave her her name back.

"Magdalena," I said, "why don't we go inside the drugstore and look for a funnel so you can uh, pee easier."

She said okay, but they didn't have anything except a catheter. I said why don't you use that? She said fuck you.

Things were getting tense.

One afternoon when we were taking a slower route through some town, for I think I must've been able to comfortably handle 40 mph by this time, a guy in a family van jumped out of his driver's seat at the red light and ran up to me waving his arms. "You dropped something a few miles back!"

I lifted up the visor on my helmet. "What?" And I could barely hear above the sounds of engines around me and cars crossing in the other direction.

"You dropped something from your bike back there!"

"Oh shit. I did?"

"Yeah!"

"How far back did you say?"

"A few miles!"

"What?" The cars in the other direction had thinned to a stop and people were revving their engines so we'd move. I didn't care. I'd dropped something off the back of my bike and they all had trunks, so they'd better chill out, dammit.

He pointed behind us. "A few miles!" and backed into his family van. I waved thanks and he nodded.

Magdalena was in front of me and couldn't really hear anything, so I motioned for her to pull over at a gas station.

She inched up beside me and lifted up her helmet: "What's wrong?"

I was looking at the back of my bike trying to figure out what was gone.

"That guy saw something fall off my bike a few miles back." My sleeping bag, tent, saddlebags. . . were all there. What was missing?

"Okay, let's go back and look—"

Then it hit me like a smack on the side of my head: "—My mother's mess kit!"

Magdalena put down her visor and started to walk her bike back. "All right, let's go and—"

"—*Not my mother's mess kit.*" And I put my bike in gear and rode right back into traffic and started scanning the road like a visual vacuum cleaner.

My mother's aluminum mess kit had been around since I was a little kid, and I remembered washing burned pancake batter off the pans in streams when I was little. The older she got, the more she was into mauve wicker tables with glass tops and the less she went camping. So it was like a passing of the aluminum Alzheimer's torch when she washed the entire set up and handed it to me the morning Magdalena and I were leaving:

"Now, remember to rub the outside of the pans with a bar of soap so it'll be easy to wash the soot off from the campfire."

★ ★

That mess kit was love, it was my lucky clam, and it was somewhere
splattered on the street. I rode on and on, faster and faster. I saw nothing but
a cruel country stretched out before me without my talisman, and Magdalena
stopped following me somewhere along the way. I knew I might have to move
into town and search for this mess kit for the rest of my life.

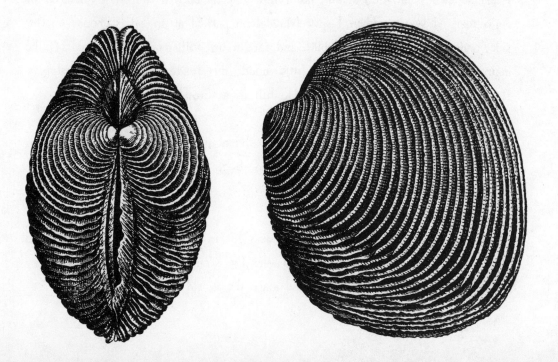

But the sides of the road were too clean. Nothing like tinfoil balls had even faked me out. I'd backtracked about five miles, and turned around in a gas station, despondent. It was gone, and I'd have to go back and tell Magdalena. I was making sure it was safe to pull out and go back, when a big blue pickup truck pulled alongside me, and a guy leaned out and asked, "Hey, you lookin' for that mess kit you dropped a little while ago?"

I looked up at them and said "Yes!"

"C'mon, follow us. We put it inside this house we're working on."

I had no idea what they meant, but followed them back a couple of miles on the main road. I waved when I saw Magdalena parked at an old firehouse on the side, and she got back on her bike and caught up with me. We turned off the main road, and down a bunch of little muddy dirt roads before we stopped in front of a house skeleton on a muddy hill in a tiny, brand-new neighborhood.

The driver got out of the truck, ran into the house skeleton and back out with my mess kit. He handed it to me, waved "bye," and climbed back in the pickup and drove off.

"Wow." I held the dented ball of my mess kit in front of me, and looked up at Magdalena. "That was amazing." It was the kind of thing that brought a blurry Vaseline mist to my eyes and made the world seem so sweet.

Magdalena wasn't smiling. Her lips were tight and she was looking at the muddy, unpaved driveway through her helmet. "Never do that again."

"What?" I got off my bike to stretch and put the mess kit back on the back.

"Just ride on without communicating with me."

"What was there to tell?" I wrapped a bungee cord through one of the major handles on the mess kit that was like a ring of Saturn. "You saw me, you decided to pull over."

"Because we had already gone three miles."

"So?"

"The guy at the stoplight told you you dropped something a few miles back." She pushed down her kickstand and swung her leg over the seat. "A few miles is three."

"What's your point?"

Magdalena stood a little straighter and put her hands on her hips. "You decided to go more than three miles on your own without consulting me. We could've been separated."

I hooked one end of a bungee cord to something and stood up. "Magdalena, you knew exactly where I was. You wanted to pull over. I went on because it's a matter of timing." I gestured at the house skeleton. "And as you can see, it was perfect."

With this much time together off our bikes, it wasn't long before we started to look at each other with contempt. She looked down at her biker boot, kicked mud, and calmly looked up at me through the tension like it was my chance to come apologize, and I was too amazed to fall on the ground and start giggling from the stress of hating her.

I reached into my pocket and came out with a little cobalt blue bottle with the name "Mister Whiskers" crossed out and "Snowball" written above it. I took one last look at it and tossed it to her.

I put the MP helmet I got for three bucks back on my head, threw my leg over my bike, pointed to myself and said, "I'm the one who hit your cat." I started the bike up and took off.

I prayed I wouldn't wipe out in the mud and fuck up this exit.

I felt a crashing punch to my head and I lost my balance. I let go of the bike and fell in the mud. Shards of blue glass were everywhere and I looked back at Magdalena. She straightened out her gloves, put on her helmet, got on her bike, lifted the visor, and yelled a bunch of stuff I couldn't understand. Californian stuff about being karmically tied to her cat, and that one day I'd pay.

Magdalena revved her engine and took off with mud flying behind her wheel, and she hairpinned out of there with her dirty belly button and flaky scalp.

Chapter Eighteen

A Crappy Time

I wanted to go home, but heading home by myself seemed like driving to Calcutta. Far away except for the nude part.

I'm not really one of the new generation that doesn't know where Vietnam is and thinks people in Calcutta are nude method actors. No. I have a shower curtain my sister gave me for Christmas that tells me where Vietnam is, and I know that people in modern Calcutta don't always fake emotions in the nude. I knew all those things, and much more in spite of my public-school education, but I don't know why I refused to just leave the bike in the mud and take the next Greyhound bus home.

Yes I do. Back when I used to run away from home a lot, I'd seen some scary Greyhound stories that made me think of the streets of England during the plague: Extremely talkative passengers with bad breath who tried to convince you to accept Jesus and scream at homosexuals; newlyweds with curious growths on their faces who got stoned in the back of the bus; and cranky, yellow-stained, and evil bus drivers who left passengers in the middle of nowhere after coffee breaks. . . passengers running behind in a cloud of dust, waving and screaming at them to stop.

Yeah, yeah, yeah, all God's creatures are great and stuff, whatever, but I felt safer leaving the bike in the mud and squatting in this shell of a house. I had a mess kit and I could pull off window molding for firewood. I could mime for money and pretend I was a robot trapped in a box until I had enough change to buy a car and drive back home.

Down the hill on the paved road, a little kid rode by on a shiny bicycle. The kind of little kid in a baseball hat who looked like he was from the back of a box of Cheerios and I felt this was the kind of neighborhood that'd lynch me for bringing down the property values, so I picked up my bike and decided to keep going west. / *Fucking WEST young lady. . . Miss Jolene Gertrude Rodriguez.*

Remember when you didn't vacuum the living room thoroughly and your mom yelled your entire Christian name? That was really very scary. Well, that's kind of how I heard my name then, standing there in the mud. It wasn't like the usual shrieking parental voice in my head, it was more like a gentle nasal breeze, and for a second I wondered if my childhood guardian angel, "Chiquita," had come back to help me.

Speaking of gentle nasal breezes, when I was a tiny little kid, maybe four or five, I used to think that when my nose did little whistles, that there were little tiny nuns singing in my nose, and my nostrils were the church. Even now I can see how two triangular nostrils can look like big windows in the front of the church. And I thought the nuns were gentle and beautiful, singing little songs, sometimes like a big chorus in my nose.

I didn't know I was just a snotty little kid who would lose all this beauty once I learned how to blow my own nose.

And then I forgot about it all and drove my bike down the future lawn.

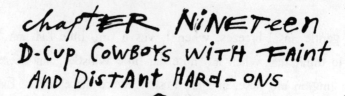

chapter NiNETeen
D-Cup Cowboys WiTH FAint
AnD DisTAnt HARd-ons

That first night alone, I didn't know what town I was in, and I didn't care. I just knew it was west.

I went to a $17 motel, where they made up for cheap rates by charging too much for their postcards, and I pushed my bike through the door of my room. The Pakistani manager seemed concerned, but I smiled and waved a lot. It wouldn't have been so bad if I'd lubricated the doorway, or taken my sleeping bag, saddlebags, and backpack off the bike, but that was the whole point: I didn't want to leave a loaded bike outside, and to unpack and pack was two hours work I wanted to avoid. I had to climb over the bike seat to get from the doorway to my bed, but it was a small price to pay to take a hot shower, turn on the air conditioner full blast, and jump up and down on the bed nude while watching bad American comedy movies on cable.

Let me tell you: D-cups are not designed to jump up and down on beds. They're also not designed to run after buses or to hurry up for anything. And you know a D-cup woman is having an absolutely fantastic time when she's on her back and doesn't lock her arms to her side to keep the cleavage alive.

In regular life, I never looked at my watch much. And on the road, I didn't seem to look at it at all, but I kept it on so I'd get one hell of a good tan line.

That, along with heading west, was all I cared about. I didn't care about America's post offices, people, pets, American valleys, rivers, streams, mountains, plains, or American miracles. I just gritted my teeth and fought the wind as I passed all those eighteen-wheeler trucks, and kept my eyes on the lines in the road while singing public-domain songs like "Happy Birthday" and "Greensleeves."

I only looked at the watch once in the morning right before I hit the highway. I figured how far I should get on the map by just after sunset so I could have my tent up and be pulling out my sleeping bag by about eight-thirty, a quarter to nine. Nice fuckin' theory.

The second night, I was just groovin' with my freedom and singing "The Star Spangled Banner" in my helmet, glad this highway was all in a straight line. I didn't think about where I was gonna sleep until it was almost dark. Checking the map, I picked the next little teepee. It was farther than I thought.

I ended up going up a mountain, via back roads in the total fucking night without a moon, trying to hack through the black fog with one wimpy headlight. I swear it took me over two hours to go thirty miles—north*east*—to the only fucking campsite around. This was supposed to be freeing.

Romantic.

I was supposed to have a heart of gold and feel like a weathered cowboy with a faint and distant hard-on./What a fucking gyp. The only time I got that feeling was my first sweet-smelling night without Magdalena.

So I learned the hard way, when the sun was low enough in the sky to make me squint (around seven o'clock), I'd look for the beginning signs to some national park 100 miles away or so.

CHAPTER TWENTY
"Zip-A-Dee-Do-Dah"

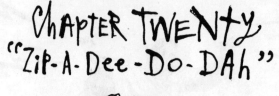

Aha!—I made it to Virginia with white knuckles, clenched teeth, and a heartbeat that sounded like kids running down the stairs. I don't think I would've made it if I hadn't started singing really loud original folk songs in my motorcycle helmet over and over. "Greensleeves" and the national anthem can only make you more crazy. They're good songs in a terrifying pinch, but I refused to rely on them.

I put the clear plastic visor down and bam. I had my own recording studio and a voice that rivaled Ethel Merman's.

> oh yeah, a kid in the country and a bottle of ale
> don't care if I'm writin' to my lover in jail
> come and see me dance
> you won't have another chance

I was thinking that by the time I made it to California, I'd have an entire album written and ready to record, go on Terry Gross's "Fresh Air" show on public radio, and she'd interview me. I'd never say "uhm" and be really relaxed and intelligent in that public radio way. With a $50 FM voice I'd say, "Why yes, Terry. I started out as a modest and inspired genius by screaming thirty-two-part harmony folk songs in my motorcycle helmet when I was riding across bridges."

sometimes you're evil
sometimes you're nice
when you beat up a nun
you gotta pay the price

oh yeah,
a kid in the country and a bottle of ale
don't care if I'm writin' to my lover in jail
come and see me dance
you won't have another chance

so give me a pot of rice
and the story of Christ
sing me a song
short or long

cause I got a kid in the country and a bottle of ale
don't care if I'm writin' to my lover in jail
come and see me dance—

(VROOOM!)

My songs stayed original until trucks sped by, leaving me swerving, and then I'd find myself screaming the *"this'll be the day that I die"* line from "Miss American Pie" in thirty-two-part harmony over and over again until I screamed the national anthem and made myself stop. . .

Zip-a-dee-do-dah, zip-a-dee-ay, my oh my what a wonderful day. . .

CHAPTER TWENTY-ONE
WAXY CHAPSTICK KISSES THAT ~~ALSO HEAL~~

I didn't give a shit what that last gas station attendant believed. I knew that as I was riding down the highway, I felt a mysterious presence over my shoulder. Screwing up my courage, I turned to look behind me and saw the translucent dead cat, Snowball, bobbing in the air behind me. The gas station attendant suggested maybe I'd ridden too long, maybe all the diesel fumes were getting to me, or maybe it was that time of the month—

"Oh yeah? Well maybe it's that time of the month for you to die!" I pushed my face in front of his and poked at his chest. After the manager came out and escorted me back to my bike, I suddenly remembered Magdalena's final Californian words about karma.

I was Snowball's killer and what Magdalena said about Snowball and me being karmically tied to each other must've been true. But Snowball couldn't have come back to haunt me. It was all a mistake. What about all that stuff my therapist said about Snowball forgiving me? It made a lot of sense and not just because I wanted it to so I wouldn't be haunted by a dead cat.

A makeshift seance is what was needed. So I said to the manager standing there that I had to go to the bathroom and he said to make it quick, so I ran into the bathroom, leaned against the wall, and lit a match. I turned out the light and closed my eyes.

"Come in Snowball, come in. Give me a sign that you hear me." Outside somewhere I heard a car start up so I continued. "Okay then, I don't want you to feel hatred toward me. If you're gonna hang around, then be like my guardian angel and I will ride this motorcycle for you because I will let you live through me and do the things you were never able to do as a cat, envying our opposable thumbs. We'll visit America's post offices together, and maybe even have sex with a stranger or watch a movie. If this arrangement works for you, give me a sign. . ." I held my breath, heard nothing, and then I heard a car accelerate away.

One of the advantages to being alone is that you're more open to the magic that's really still out there.

When I was a kid, probably around the same time my sister had her witch friends, I had a guardian angel I named "Chiquita" because I wanted to get in touch with my Puerto Rican heritage and have a Puerto Rican guardian angel, and the only Spanish word I knew was from the bananas, so I called her "Chiquita." My childhood guardian angel wore fruit on her head, felt sorry for me like a tragic TV show, and got me out of all sorts of scary shit.

As I got older and too cool for her, she packed the fruit in her suitcase and moved on.

Now Snowball's here and she will watch out so that I don't get splattered by an even larger scooter like a truck. It's all so beautiful, really.

I never met anyone who actually really and truly finished the book, *Zen and the Art of Motorcycle Maintenance*, but at least in the first 700 pages he had this smart Greek prophet guy named Phaedrus riding around in his head, telling him theories of romantic and classical people, and which type gets off on changing their own oil. Being of Zen mind, he's supposed to sound like he's not judging, but he barely hides it with a sheer veil of contempt for those who prefer to pay someone for exceptional customer service.

Maybe you're assigned a Greek prophet or a guardian angel by the motorcycle gods for when you're on the road. It does sound more like a nonprofit heaven-thing. Who gets the prophet, and who gets the angel?

As usual I wanted both, so I decided to force myself upon my angel, aware there might be biblical retribution for not accepting Snowball as she was. That was a chance I was willing to take because I needed all the help I could get. To show my confidence in her ability to be a Latin-speaking prophet, I would call her Snowballus, and if she had cat children, and there were more, I would refer to them as Snowballae. But now she was one, and she would be Snowballus: my guardian angel and my Greek prophet.

My little cat guardian angel made me feel safe, and I wanted to ask her to start holding things for me in her little transluscent paws. Like asking your mother to hold your licorice, or leaving an earring or a pregnancy test on a brand-new lover's night table so he or she has to call you back.

chapter TWENTY-TWO
BLAh BLAh BLAh

Freud didn't know how fucking right he was when he discovered that death wish/suicidal urge in people that makes them want to miss a step and tumble down into the Grand Canyon.

"C'mon. . . Jump. . . Jump. . ." It whispers like a very large baking pan. It's hard to be free / I'm so scared to do whatever I want. It's like the gravel in the road or the oil slicks and trucks that I've never actually experienced crashing into myself, but other people have warned me about. I'm afraid of crashing yet I want to blaze through life, so I live by pithy double-dare one-liners that I pull into as parking spaces, but can't back out of.

"CARPE DIEM!"
"DO IT NOW. DON'T FACE A LIFE OF SOMEDAYS!"
"FACE YOUR FEAR AND FREE YOURSELF!"
"LIVE LIKE IT'S THE LAST DAY OF YOUR LIFE!"
"KNOCK THREE TIMES ON THE CEILING IF YOU WANT ME!"

These one-liners become platitudes fast because so many of us are so fucking miserable that we print them on tea bags until we roll our eyes and go "whatever." Thoreau on a bottle cap and Confuscious on your sandwich wrapper./ We even commercialize hope.

Snowballus can spit out prophet one-liners like an improvisational gumball machine outside a supermarket, and she conveyed this idea to me: BELIEVE <u>NO ONE</u> (a *lot* of people pull into pithy statements they can't back out of).

Truth is probably something you knew all along but forgot, so you might not really have to listen to anybody else after all. Everyone should get a Greek persona and blame everything they say on it.

There is this myth that if you're a woman traveling alone people will instantly want to kill you. This is an example of where you shouldn't listen to anybody. So much of the way we live and the decisions we make in this world are based on fear. It's amazing.

Sure bad things happen. They always have.

Someone once wrote something about <u>one person</u> being cool, but <u>many people</u> are assholes. And that's the truth. A lot of times getting an asshole one-on-one is better than a group of people you love carrying ice cream.

Ice CREAM=TORchES

And check it out—I highly doubt you'd find a *traveler* pumping you full of psycho-killer fear. No. Only people who stay at home and watch too much TV will pump you full of that shit. How the fuck do <u>they</u> know? Look at their doors: they probably have fifteen deadbolts and an alarm system to protect their rhinestone-horse sweatshirts.

And one thing that won't work on the road is *acting vague*. Vagueness isn't cute on a woman away from home and it can get you involved in some cute misunderstandings. / Basically, don't giggle when you say, "I don't know."

I talk to anybody. I forget I'm a girl, and I'll go out with some truckdriver I met on the side of the road and have a few beers. And when he smiles at me with that glassy-eyed look that says he wants to blow out his chakras, and invites me to the back of his cab, I go "Yeah, sure, right. That's *real* classy" and wave good-bye.

The louder you laugh and the farther apart you plant your feet, the more respect you'll get. Take up space because it's not a school dance.

CHAPTER twenty-three
NAKED METHOD ACTORS AND THE RUMORS STARTED ABOUT THEM

I'd ridden down Highway 81 just to some state park in the bottom part of Virginia and I couldn't believe I was alive. Riding a motorcycle on a highway felt so unprotected, like being a naked method actor running alongside trucks and Pintos with forgotten turn signals.

I was the only *motorcycle* I'd seen, and I was starting to feel pretty suspicious about the whole thing. Like maybe bikers had their own private maps to other roads, and maybe I didn't have the map because I wasn't a *real* biker.

Or maybe there weren't any other motorcycles because they were already dead. . . maybe they'd already crashed into cars who cut them off without turn signals, and maybe they became road kill to be rushed off the highway by a mob of naked method actors from New York who thought wasted road kill was obscene. Would they have "tofu sucks" tattooed on their chests? Were there a bunch of witnesses back home screaming like Elizabeth Taylor about what happened suddenly this summer?

Maybe. Maybe not. One thing for sure, I was on a road that only truckdrivers seemed to know about. I'd gotten up to seventy, sometimes seventy-five miles an hour, screaming folk songs again just so I could get it all over with.

I rode up to the park office with a sigh of relief that resembled an asthma attack, and considered moving there so I wouldn't ever have to leave and get on my bike again. I found a campsite and bitched to the girl behind the counter for having to pay $15 for it. For 15 bucks I wanted a houseboy and a jug of wine.

Then I went outside the park office, called in for my messages on the pay phone and wrote a whole lot of really important numbers down on the park brochure, which I would later burn along with all my maps, as I tried desperately to start a campfire. After burning every business card in my wallet, and all the lint in my pockets, I got a fake log from the grocery store a few miles away.

I also called the Sex Toy office because my dad didn't have a phone in his hotel room. Hodie picked up the phone because as usual, she was working late.

She said he was in the hospital, but that he'd be fine. He was looking forward to my coming there because he wanted to go back East with me on the back of my motorcycle. One of the buildings actually responded to his fax about being a super.

I asked for the number to the hospital, but Hodie said they don't want him taking any calls. I said okay, fine, and we said bye.

I rode around looking for the most perfect $15 campsite that could ever be found. If I couldn't have the boy or the wine, I wanted a crystal chandelier hanging from a tree. By the time I settled on one near a little brook, it was real dark and I had to put up my tent by the light of a flashlight clutched in my crotch.

I threw my sleeping bag into the tent, jumped in, and zippered the tent up before any mosquitoes could get in.

I looked on the map, and I'd only gone an inch-and-a-half across America. I couldn't believe I'd only experienced an inch-and-a-half of pain. Eleven inches would destroy me. So I rocked back and forth, combed the knots out of my intestines while singing "Have You Ever Been Mellow" until someone yelled nicely for me to shut up.

I was tired anyway, so I burrowed deeper into my sleeping bag and thought, okay, you're near a classic babbling brook, now make sure you listen to it and appreciate it for a while.

(listen, listen)

(listen, listen)

But how long is a while? What's respectful?

(listen, listen)

Okay. That's enough.

—No. That was too fast.

(listen, listen)

Okay, how's that?

(one more listen)

Good. That was good enough.

I appreciated it for a couple more minutes before I started thinking about the fact that I hadn't filed my taxes in two years and fell asleep.

> I had this dream that I wrote a letter on a plastic liter of soda. 7-Up. And I wanted to send it to Italy or something. To someone important. And I wanted to send it immediately, but I realized the day's mail left already. Man, was I ever frustrated. But then a waiter wearing a white apron and carrying a maroon tray came to my house and asked, "By any chance, do you have any mail you want to go out? The post office really needs some mail to deliver." Boy. Was I ever glad. What a lucky, lucky day.

I woke up, and I was so excited I could actually remember a dream. I analyzed it during the entire two hours it took me to repack my bike. I couldn't even remember the last time I dreamt, and I attributed my new AWARENESS to sleeping next to the classic babbling brook.

I checked the air pressure in my tires and waited for some insights.

And as I put on my leather jacket, I thought I got an insight, but it went by so fast I missed it.

By the time I put on my helmet and saddled up on my bike, I realized the dream was about my profound love for the United States Postal Service.

But that wasn't the insight, it was just something I noticed./Didn't count.

See, I write many letters, but people call me back long distance. Usually they leave messages on my answering machine so I have to call them back long distance. And they are smart. They tell me when is a good time to reach them, so I have no excuse for getting away with my own one-minute answering machine call back to them.

I just wish people would write back for a few minutes and 32 cents.

I don't think they truly understand the joy of writing a letter on cool paper, putting it in an envelope, and addressing it in a funky way that challenges postal workers. The stamp validates the whole thing somehow, and whew!—Putting it in the mailbox and hearing that blue metal flap swing shut is just about the prettiest sound in the natural world. /The universal sound of closure. And a canceled stamp is just about the prettiest *sight*. It's almost love, and sometimes it really is love. (Unless it's a val-u pak of coupons.) It means someone thought of you for more than the fifteen seconds it took to dial your number and leave the message for you to call them back.

Plus mail is such a good deal.

The postal service is amazing and I love everyone who passed that social-service test.

As I put the key in the ignition, I make the decision to never get in that telephone message trap again. I will write them a postcard that says, *"Hey, write back."*

But my bike won't start /
it won't start /
and it *really* won't start.

I sat at the picnic table, twisted open a warm beer, and waited for the motorcycle to heal itself. A flying ant with pincers landed on my chest and I brushed him off. He landed on the table writhing. I'd fucked him up. I felt really bad because I couldn't fix him with little ant tweezers and an ant cast, and it's not like they have a little ant hospital with little ant doctors that can rush over and bandage him up.

It reminded me of the time when I was walking along the beach at the Jersey shore at night, and I saw a little crab struggling by himself in a patch of grass on a dune. I said, "I'll save you, little lost crab!" And I picked him up with a couple of sticks so he wouldn't pinch me, and walked out to the water. I wanted him off the sand so he'd be safe from the seagulls, so I walked out as far as I could on the slippery rocks and carefully held out my arms to drop him

in the right place. But he held onto the stick with his claw, and when he let go, he fell into a big wave that crashed him against the rocks.

I looked at the little ant and tried to get him upright with the end of a match in the hopes that he'd take off, but he twisted on the picnic table in agony. So I looked away, screwed up my courage, and mashed him as quick as I could with the bottom of my beer bottle.

I thought, "Aha. No wonder I couldn't appreciate a babbling brook. I am pure evil." Now I was also karmically tied to a translucent bug with pincers. How many other unknown little critters were there? Screaming spiders washed down the drain with an everyday American shower. . . ? Ever since *Charlotte's Web*, I loved spiders and felt connected to them through the plight of Charlotte.

I sat on the picnic table for three hours staring at my bike and thinking about all the animals that had died in my care, and how even when I was eight I thought I was the Antichrist because of it. / I had *always* Known. /

When the movie *The Omen* had come out, I'd identified with Damien, a little kid. He was surrounded by all these people jumping out of windows, falling down flights of stairs, or getting their heads cut off all because he wanted to be left alone to watch cartoons and eat ice cream. I stared at all the splattered bugs on the front of my dead bike and it started to rain.

Since staring was only making things worse, I walked down the road to the little campers' store where the owner said "shucks" a lot. His name was Arnold T. Smithers, and he smiled and loped around to the back of his store and came back with two clean-cut fifty-year-old Canadian bikers with beer cans in their hands. They were both named "John."

ChAPteR TweNty-FouR
ThiNgs THAT SeeMED
Like A gOOD iDEA at the
Time

Both biker Johns stood like their grandmother told them to put their shoulders back, and wore multicolored leather riding suits like Evel Knievel. The dark-haired one said, "*Hallo.* What seems to be the problem?"

(So *proper.*)

I told them my bike wouldn't start, and they spent the next two hours trying to figure out what was wrong.

The park rangers stopped by to see if we needed a battery jump, neighbors stopped by to see if they could get us anything, and camper guys cleared their throats and tried to move wires around.

When everyone gave up and left, the dark-haired Canadian John went back to the store to drink more beer. The light-haired Canadian John stayed behind and tried to figure things out. He moved slowly and I watched him talk to himself. I thought: "he'd probably be good in bed."

Fifty-four years old and Canadian. / I could already hear the classical music, the fine wine, and a leather reading chair. / Sexy and intelligent like public television.

The bike wasn't gonna go anywhere on its own. He invited me back to the store for a beer, and Arnold T. Smithers offered to let me tow my bike to a mechanic with his truck the next day.

He couldn't drive the truck himself because he was legally blind. So he got around by driving a tractor back and forth from his house to his store. Arnold T. Smithers's southern accent was so strong, I couldn't understand him much of the time.

He said, *If—If a bullfrog's butt weren't so low to the ground he wouldn't bump it so much.* I don't know what that means, but he said it for no good reason.

The Canadian bikers had come down to Virginia from Canada just to ride these mountains for a weekend. We sat back, had some beers and the dark-haired Canadian John kept telling the quieter light-haired Canadian John jokes about having sex with sheep: "Why do Scotsmen wear kilts?—Because sheep can hear zippers a mile away." I figured it was a Canadian thing. Like how inbreeding jokes are a southern thing and second date U-Haul jokes are a lesbian thing.

The Canadian John who talked to himself, the one who acted sexy in a public television way, took me for a ride on his little red crotch-rocket motorcycle / it was so amazing. I don't know what speed we went in general, but we went 70 mph just around the fucking *curves* on the switchback roads up in the mountains. A few times we were angled over so close to the ground, my right foot peg scratched the road and I was like "big deal." My left leg got pretty tired because there wasn't any foot peg on that side and I had to hold my leg up and against the bike. He'd wiped out a couple days earlier and ripped the foot peg off.

I could look out and see nothing but layers and layers of green mountains like cardboard stage sets, with little toy cows below. I held on to his back real hard-like because I wanted to have sex with his butt.

And when this Canadian John stopped in the valley below, turned around, and asked me in his proper Canadian accent if I'd like to go back with him to his motel that evening, I said, *"Fuck yeah!"*

But then he started back and I thought, oh shit. I've done it again. I only want to have sex with this Canadian guy when we're going seventy miles around curves, not when he turns around.

I couldn't bend him over and fuck him doggy-style the way the guys in South Philly do it.

These were not the raping and pillaging kind of Canadian guys. They were family men who had desk jobs, lived with lawns, and I was their *Stranded Biker Girl Experience*. The kind of memory that'd enable them to drink really bad American beer and go:

"John?"

"(*heh heh heh*) Yes. John?"

"Remember that stranded biker chick we met in Virginia when we were riding those mountains?"

"(*heh, heh*) Yes. John! Yes. I remember her. John."

"Want another beer?"

"Yes. John."

"John?"

"(*heh, heh, heh*) Yes. John?"

"Remember the time your lawnmower leaked gas all over the lawn and I accidentally threw my cigarette down?"

"(*heh, heh*) Oh yes. John. I remember that. That was pretty funny. John."

The dark-haired John always said the other John's name with a touch of sarcasm in the first and last part of everything he said. Like: "Yes. John. I love you so much I could cry. John."

Back at Arnold T. Smithers's store, I sat down, spread my knees, and leaned on my elbows. I made sure I laughed and took up space so it was clear I was in charge.

Just to be safe, I made sure I still had a couple condoms zipped up in the breast pocket of my leather jacket and the pepper spray in my right pocket.

I was so in charge as we pulled up in front of the faded brown motel and I smiled like "(ew, gross) Yes, that's really beautiful, John" and the lighter Canadian John pointed to a '76 Ford with a faded paint job and said, "That's my *hobby*." And added with a straight face, "I have a Jaguar at home." That Other car stuff is so very unoriginal.

But sometimes it still works like a charm. I once had this tiny Eskimo prostitute friend who bleached her hair platinum and carried around little metal purses which she smashed into the faces of rude men when she drank too much. Let's call her FiFi.

So FiFi worked for an escort service, and her specialty was whipping rich men near their genitalia and telling them what crappy little boys they were. They trembled in excitement on their kitchen floors and asked if she could come back tomorrow. She'd say things like fuck no, you stinky pig.

Her fantasy was to find a wealthy sugar daddy, and like my friend who found her husband in the want ads, my tiny Eskimo prostitute friend also looked in the want ads for a rich old man who wanted a tiny platinum blonde "wife." But she never found one, because I guess that kind of arrangement's just too straightforward. She should've said she liked sipping piña coladas, walking in the rain, and stepping on genitals.

Want ads are good. You can get whatever you want. Once I wanted to sell my extremely overpriced Bette Midler tickets in the want ads, and I did. I don't even like Bette Midler. I just got caught up in the frenzy of a quickly selling-out show, and I was going with a friend who adores her. I figured I should learn to love her, too. But I ask, how can you love anyone who's going to charge you $75 to watch her prance around from a crappy seat? It's insulting. Now I don't even like her more than I did before.

Anyway, one night my tiny platinum Eskimo friend got what appeared to be an average client who didn't want to cower in chains like a bad dog. He was a big, sweaty businessman who picked her up in a limousine, wanted to take her to dinner at the top of the Marriott, and just get a simple blow job afterward. She thought it was just too damn good to be true. So she was really, really nice to this guy, and pretended she was fascinated by everything he said.

After a few blow jobs, he told FiFi to leave her escort service and he would pay her ten thousand bucks a month to be his main mouth. He said he'd set her up in a penthouse apartment, and even had a Realtor show her places all over the city. He had a personal shopper scamper around for her at Nordstrom's and she looked around town for bizarre velvet furniture from Italy.

But no one could sign for the apartment or take stuff home yet, because he was waiting for money to be transferred to his Other account from his Other job in some Other city. Soon, soon. Any day now. Trust me.

This went on for about three weeks before the jig was up. He hadn't paid his $10,000 hotel bill for the suite, all the hotel dinners, and the hotel limousine. They had to pop him into jail before my little platinum Eskimo would finally admit she'd been duped first.

Three weeks of free blow jobs to a guy who looked like a big sweaty baby: it's enough to make you feel like the world owes you an awful lot.

Back in my own embarrassingly cheesy-brown low-budget adventure, the two Johns and I went into the motel room and there were two double beds. They excused themselves to brush their teeth, so I said, *fine. I need to make a few calls.* I sat down on one of the beds and called four people I knew with the hotel's name and phone number along with the Canadians' license plate numbers.

The Canadians came back out smelling like Life Savers and men's cologne, and they pulled out their badly tuned guitar and started singing Irish folk songs about falling in love with brittle-boned lasses with hair all of gold and crap.

The loud singing went on for a few hours until I couldn't smile at the mustard shag carpet anymore. I said, "I'm going to bed," and the dark Canadian John told the other John he should show me how well he sings opera, so we went out across the parking lot and he sang the theme to *The Sound of Music.* Even though I prayed for interruption, none of the brown motel curtains moved, and none of the mustard yellow doors opened. So he sang and sang like a happy little Christian, tasting every letter.

"The hiiiiills are alive with the sound of Mmmmmusic. . ."

His face turned red and with each deep breath he looked out of the corners of his eyes at me. He clenched his fists with each breath he drew in from the bottom of his lungs, and I could almost feel his pants riding up his waist as he stood there and sang how much the hills were alive with music. He tried to sing like a motorcycle ride, but it was more like a Sunday drive in a woodgrain station wagon and I thought: *I am going to fall asleep before the Canadians, and wear all my clothes to bed—even my socks.*

Around the time the operatic Canadian started singing "Edelweiss," the blood started sprinting to his face and all the crickets stopped singing because they were worried. I kept smiling like Miss America, and I turned around hoping for a complaint from the motel. But the motel just sat there the way only brown things can.

I yawned real big and stretched my arms like a fairy-tale giant: "Wow, I'm so tired, good night." I waved good-bye and walked back across the parking lot to their room in about three giant steps.

The motel room looked like a Holiday Inn's wayward brother who'd stopped caring for himself. I loved Holiday Inns. When my sister and I were little, like four and six, Mom took us to Holiday Inns when we drove that Chevy Impala cross-country. It was army green and it made us fight in the backseat just like every other kid, until Mom threatened to pull over to the side of the road and spank us with a wooden spoon or her pink hairbrush. I would swear that every time I fell asleep, they stopped somewhere so they could buy stuff for my sister. Sure, I got my share of red teepee change purses, but I know if I'd been awake I would've been able to get a teepee attaché case or the keys to a secret family house in St. Thomas.

That's where the zipper would be.

Being in a hotel or a motel was perfect living as far as I could tell. / There were no consequences. If you left a towel on the floor, you didn't have to pick it up. You never had to make your bed, and the sheets never smelled like sweat. Always fresh and white. I liked the paper band that was like a toilet hymen, and I got to be the macho conquistador. The mirrors in the bathrooms were so big, we foamed up shampoo in the plastic covered glasses and performed shaving commercials in front of the mirror until Mom told us to quit it.

We'd rinse out our glasses and run to the ice machines for the cans of soda that my sister and I were never allowed to drink at home.

Such debauchery. / I *still* get a thrill from fresh soda hitting a full glass of ice—I. Swear. To. God. The tiny sugar bubbles break on your upper lip, inside your nose, and you have to pull your lip down to protect your teeth from the ice.

The two Canadian Johns swaggered back in the room wearing tiny underwear and holding in their stomachs just as I was sitting on the edge of a bed pulling up my socks, and I knew they were waiting for this story to unfold like an origami whore and beat the time John might've set the lawn on fire.

The operatic Canadian John smiled at me and rubbed the gray furry stomach he was holding in. He was wearing loose white nylon panties and looked like he had a roll of toilet paper in there. I almost rolled my eyes, but instead I nodded "hello" like a passerby, and didn't realize how hard I was pulling on my sock until I heard a rip. He pulled back the starchy hotel covers and crawled into the bed I was sitting on, put his hands behind his head and looked at me with the confidence of a Canadian matador.

Wearing his red-and-white striped panties and popping open his seventeenth cheap American beer, the dark Canadian John said to the operatic John, "John, now don't mistake these for a candy cane, John." I threw my head back and cackled like it was a lot funnier than it was as I pulled back the covers on my side of the bed I was sharing with the operatic Canadian John. The dark Canadian John watched me and sighed: "Well, John, I guess she's made her preference quite clear, John." He finished the rest of his beer and padded over to his lonely, starched motel bed and pulled back the avocado bedspread.

As soon as he shut out the light between our beds, my operatic Canadian John rolled over and cuddled against me. I lay on my back staring at the black ceiling and wondered how this evening was going to turn out as if I were in the audience. When John nuzzled his leg between my jeans and tried to push his beef tongue into my mouth, I turned my head the other way and said to the John in the other bed, "So does it look like Quebec's going to finally be independent?"

I think he was glad we weren't going to be impolite and fuck each other while he was sleeping alone in the next bed. Plus, I was thinking that fucking right

134

next to someone is rude: kind of a carry-over from getting in trouble for chewing gum in class and not having enough for everybody.

We talked politics in loud voices across the room for awhile while my John was panting hard in my ear and trying to wedge his hand down the front of my jeans, but I had on a thick leather belt pulled so tight you couldn't even cram a Visa card down there. During a pause in the conversation, the lighter John rubbed against my jeans, buried his head in my neck, and moaned. I was worried the other John would feel left out, so I lifted my head up and in a loud friendly voice asked, "So. . . uh. . . how old are your kids?"

We both ignored the panting Canadian John and had a conversation about his kids, and how his only boy wanted to be a filmmaker and never wanted to learn how to ride a motorcycle because he thought it was passé. That hurt this Canadian John because he loved riding so much, that he even had that multicolored leather riding suit. His son wanted to be pale, have no muscle tone, and spend his time being a chain-smoking artist with smelly hair who lived in the dark telling people what to do.

The panting Canadian John tried to put his tongue in my ear and I asked about the daughter.

"Oh, she's about ten and she just loves riding on the back of my motorcycle."

"And what do you think about the United States' Libertarian party?"

Panting John tried to undo my belt, so I pushed his hand and kept talking.
"Well, maybe she'll grow up to get a huge rose tattoo on her arm, wear
sleeveless T-shirts over her small, flat titties, and ride on the back of some old
guy's Harley—"

"—John? John? You don't have athsma, do you John? Be careful over there,
John. Where's your heart medicine, John? I don't want to have to drive
nineteen hours home by myself, John."

I started laughing and the panting John got a little embarrassed and moved his
face from my neck so his saliva could get cold on my skin as it evaporated.

An hour passed by quietly. As soon as the darker Canadian John started to
snore, the other Canadian John confidently moved his hand slow and heavy
over my breasts.

I figured as long as I put plastic on him, it wouldn't be so bad. Besides, he'd
probably come really fast and it'd be over with soon. I started thinking about

the motorcycle ride so I could go through with it. I sat up, slipped off my shirt, and whispered like a saucy trollop: "Go get my leather jacket from the chair." He jumped up and fetched my jacket and I looked away so I wouldn't see his little white bikinis in the dark, otherwise I wouldn't be able to go through with this.

All I can say is it's amazing who you'll sleep with once the lights have been out for an hour and you kind of forget what they look like. People become ideas and you forget about the hair growing out of their nose, or the way they clear the phlegm from their throat after dinner. The pleasure you feel could be from the cleanest movie star when the lights have been out long enough or the beer has been strong enough. People are people, and they lie before you like naked, exposed chickens awaiting the approval they didn't give a fuck about earlier on the street.

But it didn't go fast. He must've had a problem with some man body organ or something, because he kept pounding away, and just when I thought he was done, he'd stop, get up, go to the bathroom, and come out five minutes later and start all over again. I quietly tried every position I could remember from every sex book I'd ever studied, and flexed every pee-holding muscle I had, but he just kept apologizing and getting back up. Finally, the fourth time he went to the bathroom, I noticed the sun was about to come up, so I put my pants back on and pretended I fell asleep.

The next morning when I was strapping my bike to the trailer-thing on the back of the truck, the operatic Canadian John gave me a sloppy kiss, and thinking he was being sexy, leered at me like a schoolyard pervert and said, "I loved *ffffucking* you. I wish I could stay a couple more days... *Yeeeeah*. I *loved* the feel of your *assss* against my *grrrroin* when I was *ffffucking* you." I nodded politely and turned away to scrunch up my face. Porn movie dialogue's even worse in real life.

chapter Twenty-five
The Downside of Trailer-Park Passion is The Shiny Acrylic Sweater That Comes With It

HAMBURGER ON BUN

1 pound ground beef	¼ teaspoon pepper
½ teaspoon salt	6 hamburger buns

METHOD: Preheat Griddle at 350°. Mix beef, salt and pepper. Shape into patties. Fry on one side until cooked half way through. Turn. Place bottom halves of buns on hamburger patties. Place buttered top halves of buns on Griddle to toast. Cook until meat is done. Serve with grilled onions and tomatoes. Cover to keep hot for serving.

I wasn't always this indifferent to love; I've been younger than twenty-seven before.

Anyway, you know how people tend to go out with people because they have something they want? Well, before I started to take my dreams into my own hands, I used to go out with people who had the kind of dreams I ignored. I found it inspiring. All during the relationship, we'd lay on the futon/bed-thing drinking coffee after sex, our bodies braided in sweaty sheets, the room smelling like French roast, armpits, open legs, and stale perfume / the room too dark to see the dead candles with cat hair stuck to them or the peeling paint in the room, and we'd stare at the ceiling when we'd tell each other our dreams and go "yeah" like we had no vocabulary.

"Oh. . . you're so great."

"Yeah. You too."

"Isn't it great when you like someone and they like you back the same, blah, blah, blah?"

"Yeah. Totally great, blah blah. . . Kind of like 'love,' or something, huh?"

"Yeah. Something like 'love.'"

"Yeah. Awesome doesn't even begin to describe you."

"Yeah, you're like more than amazing, spectacular, blah blah blah or something. This is cool. . ."

"Blah."

And once we break up I'd feel like an undesirable loser. See, I hate to quit even shitty jobs. I'd rather get fired. I'm the same with crappy relationships. I'm not good at that closure-thing, so even when I'm ignoring them, they usually say the quitting parts. Last word./And in spite of my boredom or independence, they were all I seemed to have.

I once had a month-long affair with a married man because he rode a Harley in circles around the city. On my futon bed-thing he said to me, "So, then I want to ride my Harley up and down Lombard Street, with you on the back. . . "

I just said yeah a lot because when you exclaim at the sunset, you kill it.

I thought, *I'm sappy. I'm wading in it knee deep spitting love-letter slush and I want to be adored for it.* I traced my finger down his unfinished tattooed back and had nothing to say. Unfinished stock fantasy tattoo with a wizard in a robe on some mountain. . . he couldn't afford to finish it because he was married, had a kid on the way and made ten bucks an hour.

He was so fucking straight. He thought that by never actually fucking me, he was somehow being less unfaithful and it somehow made him feel a little better. But I loved him more for it because he was trying to be a good person. And the sex was even better than straight fucking because he tried so hard. But its being so forbidden was enough.

He was so clean. / Took too many showers before he saw me, and his breath was nothing. Not even toothpaste. I hate corporate toothpaste breath, but it would have been something.

Nothing to say / shouldn't say, because anything would be like a twenty-five cent novel and I wanted to rip off my head and throw it in the corner like a wadded-up mistake.

The reality of my pedestrian ordinariness made me feel both safe and afraid. Disillusioned. I was every cliché and loved it. Splashing around in the cynicism of my own metaphorical black turtleneck and sunglasses meant nothing.

There was a common polyester thread linking me to all the Harlequin Romance vaginas in America. We squealed at the first loving glance from our lovers and

it really sucked.

Even before that, when I was eighteen or nineteen, first year or so of art school, I wanted to be a truckdriver and wear old cowboy boots. I wanted to show up at truck stops at 3 A.M. and order hot cherry pie. Things like that.

So I worked at a gas station, graveyard shift, and this lady, Mavis, took me under her broken arm and taught me everything she knew about the gas station/minimart business. Her armpit smelled like spring flowers in the morning dew.

Regular retail teaches you to lie down on the floor like Linda Blair and let the customers gang-rape you with a plunger./Retail also forces you to thank them and apologize for screaming when they push past your cervix. But this wasn't so bad.

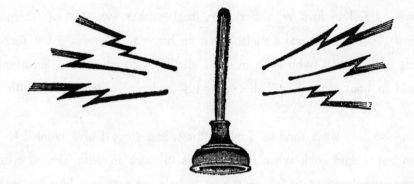

It was the middle of the night, and all we got were truckdrivers and postal workers. The postal workers gave Mavis the creeps because they were skittish and all wore the same blue chinos. The women wore them too tight so there was a big crease across their laps and the pockets opened on the side of their hips like Judy Chicago vaginas.

When they had tissues or hankies sticking out of the pockets, it was a whole other Georgia O'Keeffe floral-thing going on.

Even then, I revered postal workers. I felt like I was the only one who understood why they were always killing people. They were under intense pressure: sorting mail; reading bad handwriting; looking up postal codes inconsiderate letter writers didn't write down; dealing with upwardly mobile turtleneck catalogues; Christmas rushes; postmasters who spy on them from two-way ceiling mirrors; people who complain about a letter taking a day longer than usual; and having to fill all those little individual apartment mailboxes.

So, anyway, I fell in love with Bert. A local trucker who sort of freelanced for the post office. It seemed a match made in heaven. He was a big furry guy in his early forties who made me feel all girl. Sometimes it's important to giggle, hold in your stomach, polish your nails, and play a very polite little girl.

Well, I'm also into some kind of duality thing, and since I also wanted to be a trucker so bad, I said yeah when he asked me to move in with him. He drove his eighteen-wheeler over to the apartment to help me take out laundry baskets of my things. I admit it was over the top, kind of like trying to kill a Republican with a stake through the heart but the VW Bug I had at the time couldn't carry very much.

By nightfall, we pulled in front of his trailer home, went inside, listened to Lynyrd Skynyrd albums, ate Cap'n Crunch cereal under the neon Budweiser sign that buzzed on the wall and welcomed us home like a fat mother beetle.

When we put our empty bowls on his particle board coffee table, Bert looked at me and said: "You know, you don't have to work. I can take care of you and you could do your artwork and stuff."

"Geez, Bert, you barely know me."

"Well, I didn't say I'd marry you or anything. Not yet anyway. But you could hang out here, and uh. . . we could hang out together, and well if you wanted to or if you got pregnant, well we could get married."

"Is this some country thing?"

"Fuck you." Great. I'd hurt his feelings and he was getting a beer.

"See? We're fighting already," I said. "It wouldn't work, especially if you have to get a beer anytime there's tension. Hey, buddy, I don't plan on spending all my Wednesday nights in Al-Anon just because I happened to marry an alcoholic."

Bert turned around in the doorway. "Buddy?"

"Oh you heard what I said, my darling little alcoholic."

And we went on and on in that cycle that almost ensures that someone's going to be stalking someone by the end of the relationship.

But I've never stalked or even made crank calls. I can not tell you how many times I've been in the passengers' seats of my friends' cars as they calmly asked me to go with them to the store, only to find we were going in the opposite direction.

It was when I noticed their eyes darting like chain-smoking rats hunched over the steering wheel that I realized they hadn't heard any of my knock-knock jokes. I'd been laughing all by myself./Marlboro Lights ignored me and scanned for certain cars that were supposed to be in certain parking spaces or certain lamps turned on in certain rooms. By the time they'd broken into the cars and started sniffing the seats, I strongly suggested we leave. I was a real good friend. I'd push the broken glass under the car so as not to alert passersby walking their dogs and I'd always put the brick back in our car in case they scoured for fingerprints.

So here I was with my own man to stalk / going through the frenzy of my twenties. We were supposed to mow lawns together, and panic set in about being alone as if I'd never done it before. But like everyone else, we caulked over the potential mold of our relationship and before you could say "get me a beer, hon," we were back in each other's arms and he was calling me his trailer-park girl.

A couple of weeks later I found myself in the beauty parlor wearing skintight white Lycra pants and a turquoise sweatshirt with rhinestones in the shape of a horse. I was asking how much it would cost to get my nails extended and painted with rose decals on the tips. I wanted to belong / look like the other women in the grocery store. I accidentally looked up and saw my reflection in

146

the huge mirror tiles on the wall, and somewhere in the back of my mind I heard someone beating on the soundproof glass that separated the right and left sides of my brain.

I didn't know it then, but that someone was my old guardian angel, Chiquita, come back to save me, reminding me of when I was twelve and started hanging around Puerto Ricans because I wanted to be one. Everyone's mom had shaved off her eyebrows and drawn thin black lines far above where they used to be. I'd wanted to shave my eyebrows off, too. To be free of their expressions so I could make up my own.

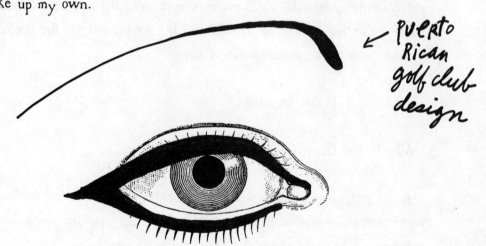

← puerto
Rican
golf club
design

And it hadn't even been 1974. It had been more like 1981 or something, so there was no excuse. Anyway, my eyebrows never totally recovered. Afterward, I feared that I might have to Scotch-tape fresh caterpillars to my face every day.

In my head I turned away from the gold-toothed beautician smiling at me, and saw Chiquita throw her body against the glass the instant before it shattered. Chiquita yelled, "Remember the Ronald McDonald eyebrows!" Everything clicked like a clock striking high noon, and I ran out of the beauty parlor in my white spike heels.

I went back to the trailer and mechanically opened up some canned asparagus, fried up some Spam and made some Kraft macaroni and cheese. By the time Bert got home and kissed me hello, I'd forgotten to heat up the asparagus so I put it on the plate cold. We ate in silence until the both of us finally looked up at each other. Without another word, I got up and got the box of Cap'n Crunch, some milk, and a couple of bowls.

"Bert, I can't do this anymore."

"What? Eat Cap'n Crunch?"

"I'm not getting any cartoons done because I'm trying to learn the best ways to serve chicken croquettes from *Woman's Day*. If I put this much into my cartoons, I'd be doing *New Yorker* covers by now."

"Hon' I've never asked for chicken croquettes."

"But I'd feel guilty living off you and hanging out all day doing my own work."

"I like fish sticks."

"Fish sticks?"

"Yeah." Bert topped off his bowl with Cap'n Crunch and started reading the back of the box.

"I hate fish sticks. I don't even like tuna fish, Bert. We're gonna starve. I need protein or my face is gonna start hanging. Look at this cupboard. Look. With food of this nutritional value, I'm sure to age fifteen years in another two weeks. God. I already feel like I'm forty-five. By the end of the month I'll be sixty, and this lady down at the parlor turned forty and she said her husband had said he was gonna turn her in for two twenties and you know what?"

Bert grunted and ate another spoonful of cereal.

"He did. Last week he left her for two twenty-year-olds. And at the end of the month when my skin's hanging and my eyes are yellow and my hands are covered with liver spots, you're not gonna love me anymore. Then you'll start having affairs with some young dispatcher at work. You'll imagine her holding that steel gray phallic microphone day in and day out, and you'll get hard simply hearing her voice over the loudspeaker as you load smooth and mysterious U.S. mail on your truck. With every load you lift, you'll fantasize about all the mail you could send to each other. I'll start getting needy and bitchy, and start wearing way too much makeup. . . I won't even care if the cellulite on my legs show through the skintight leggings I wear in public."

I looked at Bert with watery eyes and sat down in front of him. I moved the Cap'n Crunch cereal box that was a barrier between us and gently held his hand. He put down his spoon, looked up at me and asked:

"How did you know about that dispatcher at work?"

Wow, I was nuts, man. I was close to having a fucking *garden* for this guy. Yeah, I would've worn an apron, made bread, and popped out kids like tiny shiny Life Savers. And if it weren't for the Jif peanut butter and too much Cap'n Crunch, I probably would've been happy. Something about that scares me. What exactly, I'm not sure: actually being happy, or that being a homemaker would've made me happy.

I would've gone around a braless earth mother, listening to folk on the old record player, nursing my little kid, looking all peaceful next to my garden of sunflowers and fresh tomatoes. My hair would've had natural highlights. I'd have no split ends and I'd get those cool crow's feet in the corner of my eyes from being in the sun so much. And I'd be really dark. I wouldn't care about the fact that my *chocha* was just sewn back up, or that my urethra muscles were so fucked up I'd pee myself everytime I laughed. It wouldn't be so bad except for the fact that I laugh a whole lot. I'd have to wear Depend adult diapers for the rest of my life.

That's so damn sexy. I could masturbate right now.

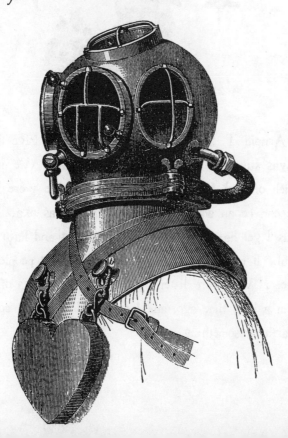

chApter twenty-six
A Little Black Kid Can't Bleed on TV Without Looking Like a Stereotype

Legally BLIND Arnold T. Smithers and I were left to drive the bike to the mechanic who was supposed to be fifteen miles away. We drove for an hour on a whole bunch of back roads before he admitted we were lost. Looking for a parking space can be an adventure for me, so it was okay. The land was so beautiful, plus I get happy when I smell cow shit and hay. And horse shit is just wonderful. It means I'm not in the city smelling people shit. People shit is pretty horrible. / We were listening to eight-track tapes of Hank Williams's greatest hits from a long time ago, and I was into it. I felt cool, like I was truly down-to-earth or something.

Finally we found the place and I felt like Moses in a four-cylinder pickup truck. A big barn on the top of a hill in the middle of nowhere and a whole herd of dead old motorcycles sat in the field like exhausted cattle. We pulled up in front of the door and got out.

This guy named Dave came up to us wearing his mechanic's blues and a baseball cap. He smiled when I told him *my* bike was dead. He walked around to the bike, looked at the New Jersey tags and asked me if I'd actually ridden this thing from New Jersey all by myself. I could barely understand his accent and Arnold T. Smithers smiled proudly for me with his hands in his pocket, rocked back and forth on his feet and answered, "Why, yes. Yes she did."

Dave looked at my tits a lot because I had this cotton shirt on with heavy shell buttons that made the first button sag, so the shirt opened a little gap at the top. You couldn't even see anything. Just a little skin. But it's kind of like the Victorians putting skirts on the bottoms of sofas so they couldn't even see the suggestion of legs. A little skin showing where it's not supposed to might get you a price break, and I was still feeling a little whorish anyway, so I pushed my hair behind my ear and smiled at him.

He checked the fuel, spark and compression. Said it might need a valve job. Could run a hundred, but if the engine needed to be pulled, it could run five hundred.

153

Arnold T. Smithers and I went back and I took a long nap on the chaise longue on the back porch, waiting for anything while Arnold T. Smithers sat behind the counter in his store selling campers cigarettes, Dr. Pepper's, and Milky Way bars.

With the Canadian Johns on their way back to Canada, I was reminded that I was pretty much on my own. I felt at home with their restrained whiteness. Arnold T. Smithers kept on telling everyone how I reminded him of his daughter. I couldn't figure out how since he'd said his daughter had four kids, and even though she only lived six miles away, wasn't talking to him.

I have only seen two black people during my stay down here. Then we turned on the TV in the store and on the news they said a motel got robbed. It was done by two black guys and they put their pictures on the screen./That made four black people.

Arnold T. Smithers had a house right next to his store, but his wife was staying there and she wanted a divorce because she said she just didn't love him anymore. Simple as that. He was kind of bummed and he didn't know what he was gonna do. He was in his mid-fifties, but pretty sickly so he looked like he was seventy-five. Everything was in his wife's name and he wasn't sure he even wanted to keep the store anymore because he had these blind spots that were like when a BB gun shoots through a window. He kept giving back the wrong change.

He had two cabins which he rented to vacationers, and he was staying in the basement of one of them. He said if I needed a place to stay, I could stay there with him. He had a sofa bed.

His cat hung out with me on the back porch of his house, and Arnold T. Smithers said he liked to feed his cat fish, but it gave him the back door trots. And when he used to feed it to him twice a day, he was spraying like a squirt gun and never quite made it to the litter box.

Dave at the bike shop called back at the store and told me it just needed the valves adjusted. I'd have to hang out with Arnold T. Smithers for a few days in his basement, but that was okay with me. The longer I was off that bike the more I was sure I didn't want to get back on.

I pulled out my map and looked for the tiniest roads that were the widths of baby hairs. When I added up the mileage I figured I'd make it to California in a little under eight months. I didn't have enough credit on my secured credit card to last me more than two months. Especially after the valve job that was gonna run me a hundred. I took another nap on the chaise lounge with the cat who couldn't eat fish, and waited until ten when Arnold T. Smithers closed the store and took me back up to his basement on the hill.

★ AND ★

The basement was damp, chilly, and covered with fluffy little bathroom rugs in dusty pink, forest green, ocean blue, and refrigerator yellow./Last Tuesday's salad.

The first thing Arnold T. Smithers did was empty the dehumidifier.

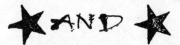

Arnold T. Smithers and I hung out a lot at his store and he showed me how to play pool. I hadn't played since I was seven and hanging out in Montana for a month. I'd worn a cowboy hat and told everyone to call me Joe. I'd played the part of a boy real cool until this other little boy named Eric showed me how far he could pee over the hood of a car. It totally freaked me out, and then I wasn't a boy anymore. I watched cattle getting branded on the ranch where we were staying and I cried through the entire thing. The ranch smelled like burning flesh and rotting meat to me because even the house cats were gutting small animals and leaving the gassy entrails rotting in the barn.

So there I was playing pool with Arnold T. Smithers in his little store and he was letting me win even with his BB gun vision. That night when we went home to empty the dehumidifier and watch TV, he felt comfortable enough to take out his false teeth in front of me. I tried to pretend I was paying attention to the sitcom but instead I focused on his false teeth. By the time we made it through a couple of sitcoms, I flew into a depression about rotting teeth and dying and being buried and rotting underground. I'd known this Puerto Rican lady, Julie, who also had drawn on eyebrows, she had false teeth by the time she was twenty. She went to clubs a lot and said men loved it because she could take her teeth out when she gave guys blow jobs/Said she could do cool things with gums, as long as it was in the dark.

I think about death too much, even when I'm not a moving target for trucks. Everyone's supposed to have this one nightmare that's a theme in their life, a painting they paint a thousand times/a neurotic cul-de-sac. One person's obsession may be Justice—another's may be Artistic Lighting or Saving Alcoholics. Mine is Death and Time. I get two obsessions because my sun sign is Leo. I get more. Always more. / Twice the terror.

We all want to be remembered but we're not going to be. Even Bette Midler and Zsa Zsa Gabor will rot and eventually become obsolete like some sort of movie star during the Egyptian age. And if you do happen to become remembered, you will only become chipped stone with pigeon shit all over you like a statue of Marcus Aurelius. No one will remember how good your chicken was or that your house smelled like strawberry incense or throw up. None of that will matter.

No one has any pull, and I realize no one's opinion of anything really matters more than yours until they figure out how to stay alive forever. A snotty, condescending attitude—like the kind in expensive hair salons or clothing stores—might simply be an attempt by people who probably don't even have health insurance to fake you out so you think they know all the songs in The Key of Life by heart.

Sure, we may be remembered by those who love us after we're gone. But one day they're gone, too. Maybe we do everything so we'll be remembered, have some sort of control. Maybe that's why artists create things or why people kill people. Because it's like, *don't act like you know you're going to live longer than me. Okay, so I will. Bang, you are dead. I may not be remembered in a thousand years, but I killed you.*

I've got to get to some kind of spiritual point where I won't give a shit and blow through life without thinking one day these are gonna be ancient times, because this is getting ridiculous.

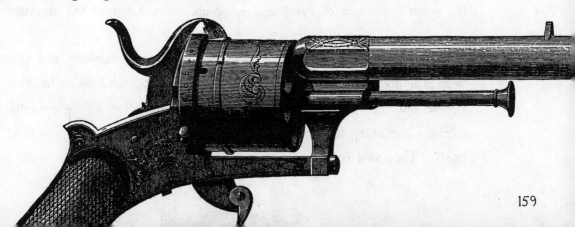

Being remembered. That's why people dress well, dress bad, that's why that lady colored her hair red to match her coat. So someone will notice her today and say, "Cool."

One day the new refrigerators or Mustang convertibles we wanted so much will just be rubble like in the ruins of Egypt. Sometimes when this cycle gets going I can't look at my own arm without seeing it old and shriveled or my face covered with age spots and sagging. I'll even look at my cat and start crying because I know I've really gotta enjoy her now. It's gotten so she can't stand being in the same room with me anymore. She leaves as soon as I sit down.

Lobotomies look good, and I'm not kidding. I've gone to sleep with images of my own skull rotting underground with worms crawling around the fillings in my teeth that I was once so upset about because they made me broken.

That's why road kill scares me so much. No matter how much we try to dress the whole experience of living and dying up, we're just road kill in August.

Sometimes I feel like I'm going insane. All the writers, thinkers, and artists I wanted to discover how they stopped being spooked by thinking in tail-chasing circles, how they got over it—I would find out they all ended up committing suicide by drinking themselves under tombstones or shooting holes into their heads. They said fuck it / what's the point.

Some people like these incorrectly thought having kids would take the fear and responsibility of living away and make their lives full of pastel hazes. But one day the kid toddles across the room and asks the meaning of life and why the sky is blue. And there you are all over again, hittin' the bottle or reaching for the gun because you don't have the foggiest idea.

And the kid grows up to tell quite a story to some ninety-dollar psychoanalyst. And as usual, Led Zeppelin was right: The song remains the same.

Sometimes when I'm less scared, I find solace in imagining I've written a book that'll be pinned down and dissected like an old frog in some future high school class. The teacher will scrape out every insignificant word like cake batter at the bottom of the bowl, look for recurring imagery and symbolism, and ask the bored students, "So, what do you think she *really* meant when she said 'crotch rot'?" The teacher will wait for an answer, but the students in the year 2090 will all be looking at the holographic clock levitating in front of the wall. Ten minutes for the bell to ring. She'll scan the room, holding a fiftieth edition of my marked up, tattered paperback to her chest, "Okay, you, Jean-Luc Picard." The teacher will point to a boy in the back whose life I've affected like a brush on the arm long after I'm beyond dust.

And what will he say?

"Engage"? / "Make it so, Number One"?

My head hurts and I want to crawl into my sister's bed like when I was little and couldn't sleep because the vastness of the universe scared me, and my brain would always be too small. But there is no bed I can crawl into anymore that'll take this full-grown horror away. / This is the loneliest feeling I can feel and it scares me to the point of wanting to smoke a clove cigarette and do something like ride across country on a motorcycle I don't know how to ride.

Here and now, here and now, here and now. I try to give myself a lobotomy with a mantra. Any mantra will do. *Watch TV. . . asses are what's important, baby veal placenta for your wrinkling eyes, your tits defy gravity and I love you for it, Gilligan, the Skipper too. . . you deserve to be kicked senseless, your armpits smell, your head is flaky and you deserve to die. . .*

Die?

Ice cream is nice. Ice cream will make everything okay.

I hate, hate, hate catching sight of celebrities in real life. Even though they're supposed to rot too, I need to maintain the illusion that there are a million copies of each actor and that they're truly the characters they play and will live forever on TV. I hope to God I never, ever run into Xena the Warrior Princess. I refuse to even watch the actress who says she plays her on talk shows because she makes me think Xena's not real. And you don't understand: Xena must be real and Xena must live forever.

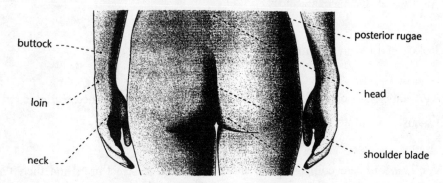

On the day my bike was ready, Arnold T. Smithers and I sat in front of his store in the sun. He said, "Well, shucks, Tomato. You'll be leaving today."

I nodded and swung my feet back and forth because they were too short to touch the ground.

He smiled. "Uh, well, I'd like to take you out to dinner. To a really nice place."

"Aw, geez Arnold, you don't have to do that. Let's just hang out and watch TV on my last night here."

"Shucks, I don't wanna make you feel uncomfortable or nothin'. I mean, well. . . if you don't have anything nice to wear, I could take you to Wal-Mart and get you a cheap dress."

I looked at him and I was a little scared inside, like he wanted me to be his new wife or something. "Oh, no Arnold. I, I really couldn't let you do that."

"An' maybe some cheap shoes."

I looked at him and swung my legs.

"Aw, shucks, Tomato. I didn't mean to make you feel uncomfortable. . . well, let's just go out to dinner."

"Well, maybe we could stop by the post office or something, and then go out to dinner, you know."

"Post office?" He looked pretty puzzled.

"Yeah. I kind of like post offices and maybe you could take my picture in front of it."

"Which one? There're two."

"The prettiest one."

He looked at the ground and rubbed his scraggly chin. "The prettiest one? I ain't never thought of which one was pertier."

"Well, you choose." I swung my legs straight out in front of me and looked up at him like a four-year-old girl with all the confidence in the world in her daddy.

Arnold T. Smithers smiled, did a definite nod, jiggled the keys on his belt loop, and said, "Well now, we have to go pick up your bike this afternoon," and he shuffled back into the store.

There was this guy living in his orange van across the street from the store and Arnold T. Smithers asked him to go with us to pick up my bike because he couldn't drive back himself.

I forgot the guy's name, but he never wore a shirt, and he had a big gut. He always had sunglasses and a fishing hat on with a pipe hanging out of his mouth. His van was the kind from cop movies in the seventies, the kind with two tinted little square windows in the back doors, except it had carpeting all over the walls and a foam mat in the back for sleeping. He used to ride around and follow the rodeos, but now he just traveled around and worked as a dishwasher in diners.

He told me to grab the plastic white lawn chair from the back porch so I could sit up in the back, and said: "Have you seen Dolly Parton's new shoes?" I said no, and he said, "Well neither has she."

165

chapter twenty-seven

Love Letters Propping Up The Corner of a Bookshelf

one less bell to answer, one less Egg to fry

Speaking of Dolly Parton, for a little while there was that rumor about her being a lesbian. I thought about having sex with Dolly Parton for a minute. And what about those wigs? She'd have to keep the wig on so you could hold onto something. The puffier and whiter, the better. And without the wig, they could just be sending in the chauffeur, telling you, yeah, sure that's Dolly. Go ahead and sleep with her.

I thought about how you probably wouldn't want to fuck things up with a woman like that. The pressure must be enormous. Geez. And then it seemed like just too much work and I looked out at all the pickups and the ranch houses on the sides of the road. I was really glad I didn't have a penis.

because you can't just lie down and fake it. Or it would be difficult. I bet you thought I was going to say "hard" instead of "difficult," huh? I'm not that cheap. But yeah, I was glad I didn't have a penis, even though I've often wanted a nice dense goatee.

If I could've grown a thick, glossy beard with touches of gray, I would've. Give me a nice goatee and I'd wrinkle my forehead in thought, say "hmmm," and stroke my beard while thinking profound thoughts. People would think I was wise and come up to ask me questions, and being truly wise because of my beard, I would have the courage to say "I don't know" when I really didn't know. And when I did know, they'd walk away with changed lives. They'd make sure their pets were always neutered and still refuse to buy gas from Exxon.

But my beard just looked scraggly like an adolescent boy's, so I put dishes of wax in the microwave to rip it off my face so I'd look good in lipstick in case I ever decided to wear any. But I hardly ever wore it, because when I did, I'd forget, wipe my mouth, and have a big red smear across my face all day.

Yikes/The thought of being a man who had to measure up. The stress alone could make you a shitty politician. Sometimes I'm such a pillow queen, I won't even masturbate. Somebody else has to do it for me. So much of the time, it's only about exceptional service.

Well, the first time I seriously approached lesbianism—beyond replaying the girl-girl scenes twelve times in straight porn—I drove my VW Bug to my mom's house in the suburbs. I paid $200 for that car, and it was great. But I got 2,300 bucks in parking tickets, and one day I went into the corner store for a pack of cigarettes and a conversation, and by the time I came back out, the car had a boot on the axle and a red warning sticker on it.

So I started taking the bus.

Anyway, before all that, I drove to my mom's, one of the times she was living with Violet. It was high suburbs, right around Thanksgiving, and all the houses on the block looked alike, so I had to slow down at the other end of the street and start looking for the only house without Thanksgiving decorations on the front lawn.

I pulled in the driveway and ran out of my VW Bug back through the comfortable doors, but my mother with very strong boundaries greeted me with raised eyebrows in the foyer: "Hi, Jolene," she said. And her eyebrows continued to say, "I'm glad to see you, but you know about calling first before coming over. I've told you about respecting our space. You know that as a family we have boundary issues."

The sting of the rubber band snapping back into place left me feeling chilly, poor, and defensive. "I know Mom. It's just that our phone was just turned off, and you know how I hate to make collect calls from public pay phones. They have grunge on the earpiece."

Mom looked at me with tight lips like I knew better and sighed. "Next time carry napkins with you."

"And Mom, call me Tomato."

"I did."

"No, you didn't. You called me 'Jolene.'"

My mom's girlfriend, Violet, coughed at the top of the stairs and slowly eased her way down like a queen. With an unlit cigarette dangling from her mouth, she eventually made it to the bottom of the stairs and lit it with the lighter on a cord around her neck. She coughed up a little phlegm into a tissue, looked at nothing in particular, and said "Hello, Jolene." Then she flashed a critical look at my mom that said, *Boundaries! What about our boundaries!* and went back to a half-lidded look at a world that wasn't nearly as exciting as cable.

My mother sighed through lips as taut and thin as dusty rose paper clips, and gently reminded her, "She likes to be called 'Tomato.'"

Violet was too tired to roll her eyes all the way, but she made a good effort and sighed for the finale.

"Now, Violet. We need to respect what our children want as adults." Mom opened up the hall closet. "Here. Hang your coat in here, don't leave it out. You know how we hate that."

"Can I put it on that hook?"

My mother sighed and slapped me with a look that said, *don't start with me, young lady. You came over here without calling first. Boundaries. . . boundaries. . . boundaries. . .*

I imagined all of us protected by invisibile squares of masking tape on the floor that followed us wherever we walked like hoop skirts, and if anyone crossed over into our space we were allowed to shoot to kill the way you can when burglars go into your house. The way I punched my sister when she put her leg over the vinyl separator in the backseat of that Chevy Impala when we were kids. I was like *fuck, you already got Mom's love and the best of the teepee change purses what more do you want, you extremely adopted little home wrecker?*

I hung my coat on a hanger, put my hands in my pocket, and nodded politely to the passing Violet. She was still in her housedress, the one with the big pocket between her huge tits. It was for cigarettes, phlegmy tissues, and phone numbers.

"How are you?" I nodded and smiled.

She moaned and coughed up some more phlegm as she shoved past us in slow motion into the kitchen. "Oh, my colitis is acting up and my back still hurts."

My mom once said that when you turn forty, your body that's been your friend forever, all of a sudden becomes your enemy and starts rotting on purpose. Your brain can't remember where you parked the car and your eyes can't read the intelligent note you wrote to remind you it's at Fifteenth and Spruce. "Wow. That sucks—" I said as sympathetically as I could, being raised by a mother who made us go to school unless we could prove beyond the shadow of a doubt that we were actually vomiting. I turned to my mom and rubbed my lower lip. "—Hey Mom, listen. Can I talk to you?"

"Yeah." She sighed and started following Violet into the kitchen. "We can talk in the Jacuzzi. My legs are really hurting."

It was good to be at home and at least feel like a part of the shrinking middle class again.

My mother came out in her bathing suit, and brought a mason jar of wine, her reading glasses, a book light, and a self-help book to the Jacuzzi on the deck in the back of the house. She climbed in, leaned her head back, and closed her eyes. I crouched around in tiny circles watching my breasts float inside my tank top, and I felt like I was in a Western with all that spontaneous cleavage / like I should be bringing some windblown cowboy a hard drink with the kind of concerned smile that wears a lot of eye liner.

"So mom, when did you know you were a lesbian?"

My mom wrinkled her forehead and sighed, because that's how she and Violet reacted to everything / even visions of the Virgin Mary in Medjugore. "Oh God. Not another one of these conversations."

"No, Ma. I'm serious."

She opened her book and looked at me over her reading glasses. "Why are you asking me this?"

I continued hopping around in circles appreciating my breasts floating in a Jacuzzi. "Because I'm wondering if I should be a lesbian. You and Violet get along so well. You both are like friends, and well, that's what I want. Like you probably trust each other and stuff. I think it's a woman thing. You both really know how to be sensitive with each other."

(swoosh—bam!) Violet slid back the sliding glass door to the deck. She had a dishtowel draped on her shoulder and she pulled the cigarette out of her mouth and yelled across the deck, "Jane! I thought you were going to buy the turkey! Where's the damn turkey?" She pulled out a tissue and coughed up some phlegm.

My mom held the self-help book from her face and yelled back, "We don't need the turkey until *Thursday!* I'll buy it tomorrow!"

"*Tomorrow?*" Violet sighed loudly enough so we could hear her across the deck.

"Yes! *Tomorrow!*"

I kept crawling around the Jacuzzi in little circles and I wondered if you were a lesbian would you still find Clint Eastwood sexy? Or would you see through his whole furrowed-brow facade but still be able to vote for him for mayor of Carmel?

"Jane. How do you expect to find a turkey the *day before* Thanksgiving? Huh?"

"Don't worry, Violet! I said I'll get one tomorrow. Do you not trust me to be responsible? How do you think I raised two kids on my own and ran an agency with fifty employees?"

"Your kids are fucked up! Your daughters show up without calling first because they have boundary issues! You can't always coddle them, Jane. How do you expect them to make it in this world without boundaries? Huh, Jane?"

"Tomorrow! I'll get a nice turkey tomorrow—*okay*, Violet?"

Violet ripped the kitchen towel off her shoulder and started waving it in the air. "Jane, this is a problem with you. You're *always* waiting until the last minute, and I refuse to let you do that with this turkey. You *know* I have food and security issues! You really let me down, Jane. My feelings are hurt and I feel angry with you." She started coughing and she reached into the pocket between her breasts and pulled out a ball of tissue and spit into it. "What do you expect me to feed everyone, Jane? Frozen dinners like you used to feed your kids?" She tucked the tissue back in the pocket.

"Hey! So you feel hurt—okay, I hear that—but I'm starting to feel discounted and attacked. *So what* if I can't cook. Get off my back!"

"I'm tired of bailing you out of your responsibilities and rescuing you!"

"*Me?* You rescuing *me?* I'm sick of rescuing *you!* Who's the one who sat down and talked to your son about his drug problem while you stayed in the bedroom and binged on ice cream sundaes until three in the morning?"

"Hey, don't talk about my boys. Leave my boys out of it! And next time you want help rearranging the furniture, don't look at me!" My mom rearranged furniture about every two or three weeks.

"And next time you want me to run to the pharmacy in the middle of the night, don't look at me!"

"Fine, Jane. If you want to start fighting dirty. . ."

"Violet, I think it's high time we make another therapy appointment! And this time, you make the call!"

"Fine. Jane. I will!"

"My appointment book's in my briefcase on the kitchen table!"

"Fine!" *(swoosh/slam!)* Violet slammed the sliding glass door shut and went back into the kitchen. Mom jerked her self-help book back in front of her face and I looked up at the stars.

"See? That was beautiful. the way you both worked that problem out." I waved my arms in the warm water like a treading fish. "I could tell you both take turns calling the therapist to make appointments and stuff. Sharing your feelings. Working tough issues out. Even though everything's not always rosy. you two have a gentler, more profound relationship than any heterosexual couple I've seen. I want that. I want to have an intense, beautiful spiritual relationship like you two.

"Can I borrow some of your lesbian information? I'm sure you have pamphlets lying around I could read. don't you?"

I hadn't really realized until I wanted to be one that Violet and my mother were pretending they weren't being lesbians. Violet was fifty-five years old. Catholic. and in denial about loving women. My mother just figured it was no one's business. So it got to the point where they were pretending they weren't "lesbians" with each other, especially because they hated the word. They thought it was harsh to the ear with the "z" crashing right into the "b" sound.

I agree. Any other word would be an improvement. Even if we called lesbians "trees" it would be better. There was no other word to use without looking like they were in denial about being lesbians, so they just said nothing at all and went about their business.

I stared over at my mom for a few minutes thinking that she was considering my question. I nudged her: "Well?" She looked over her self-help book at me and pushed her bifocals up on her nose. "What?" she sighed. "I'm sorry, I didn't hear what you were saying."

Then I went back to the city, went to the video store for a bunch of straight porn with girl scenes. I looked at the pictures on the tape cover: Mall girls with hair as big as turkeys were bouncing on each other's faces and I realized, "Wow./No more pretending semen is melted ice cream."

And for the next hour I masturbated with a roll-on deodorant bottle and came as I watched the videotape of squealing mall girls wearing too much lip gloss, fucking each other with pig-colored dildos and jerking each other off as if they were dialing telephones with wet fingernails.

Then the phone rang and I picked it up. "Hello?" I karate-chopped a soft pack of cigarettes to see if any were left. Two.

I instantly recognized the voice of the student loan lady asking if a Miss Jolene Rodriguez was at home. I said, no, she got kicked out because she didn't pay the rent, and was living under a bridge somewhere. She said thank you, she'd try later.

I hung up the phone, lit a cigarette and watched the video as one of the high-haired mall girls sucked wildly on her aerobic instructor's nipples without smearing her lip gloss, and I asked my cat, "Hey, Nena, come over here. Do you ever fantasize about something and then after you get off, think *oh that is so stupid*?"

She looked at me, and her eyes said *all the fucking time*.

chapter twenty-Eight
No, Those Aren't Panties, Those are Prayers

I went to pick up my bike, and Dave the mechanic said to try it out. I got on the bike and said don't look because I don't want to wipe out. He got in a conversation with another guy and I rode down the gravel way. I made a sharp turn off the gravel to turn around, and I wiped out on the grass and got a wife-beater bruise on my thigh from the bike landing on my leg.

I lightly yelled for help and waved.

Dave, the mechanic, ran up to me, picked the bike off my leg and said: "How in the hell did you get your motorcycle license, girl?"

"Motorcycle license?" I sounded surprised. "I didn't know you needed a special license for these things." I lied. I knew it. I didn't have one, but I knew it.

Dave, the mechanic, said he'd drive me down to the hard-top road, so he got on the bike, told me to get on back and cruised down the hill. It felt good to be driven around. He leaned back and gently leaned his head between my breasts. *That's* what D-cups are for. Not for running after buses.

I could've ridden bitch forever, but instead I became a bitch forever.

chapter twenty-nine
Liver Dancing

Aaah. Riding bitch. Next best thing to being a pillow queen, or experiencing exceptional customer service.

Except that I must admit it runs a little boring riding bitch after a while. So does being only the fucked, or the constant recipient of excellent customer service.

Something honest and real about someone finally saying fuck you, man, you're on your own.

Later on, I would find out how much girls found riding on the back of my bike sexy. It wasn't me. It was the bike, the ride. I could've been a greasy troll and they still would've played with my tits while I was driving. Like they just didn't get it.

And what was in it for me? Nothing could be less sexy than being responsible for someone else's life on a motorcycle that cars don't see. I'm paranoid about cars cutting us off and making left turns in front of me.

It's so nice to sit in a big lap and let someone else worry about changing the oil once in a while.

Chapter Thirty
Pulling My Hair Back Without any Hands

Even though I fell asleep on Arnold T. Smithers's sofa bed thinking about how it would suck once you were old and no one cared about impressing you anymore, I woke up emotionally farting and feeling financially cheap. Before I even opened my eyes, I was adding up all the times I covered things preparing for this trip with Magdalena and told her not to worry about it. *That wrench she needed, all the oil she got on my secured credit card, the loaf of bread. . .*

I took over two hours to pack up my bike and I took about eighty-five last good looks around before I set off to leave. I didn't wanna go because I had no idea how I was gonna pull this whole thing off: I'd forgotten how to ride.

I went down to Arnold T. Smithers's store and took forty-five minutes to say good-bye. Finally around two or three in the afternoon I shoved off.

On my way into Nashville with six lanes of traffic merging and the slow lane torn up with grooves and craters in the road, it started to rain. Oh, not like a gentle little cute rain, but a horizontal, crazy garden-hose rain. It stung like a thousand tiny spankings, and my lips were peeled back from my gums and I hummed crazy things through my teeth. I'd actually bought a rain suit to wear, but I was already soaked and my toes were squishy in my boots. The only thing good about this rain suit was the plastic pouch it came in. I was using the pouch for my map, which I strapped to the gas tank.

Cars were weaving in and out of lanes and I stayed in the slow lane which just happened to be going under construction. I kept close to the shoulder and watched for the potholes and grooves through what felt like seventy layers of Saran Wrap over my eyes. Cars were so sweet. I thought they'd pass me by in my own lane, but they gave me a wide berth as if they sensed my invisible masking-tape boundary. I loved them and wanted to give them hugs without crashing into their windshields.

I lived, and just past Nashville the rain let up and I pulled over to a rest stop with truckers hanging out like big metal pigeons. A self-centered minivan family was parked under the only tree available and I practically rested my bike against the van to make a point. I lit a cigarette, and it was the first time I inhaled all day. I felt my arm and leg muscles relax. I couldn't fucking believe I'd made it. The sky was clearer up ahead and I envied no one.

Not long after that, I was back on the highway going toward Memphis, and there were two lanes—I was in the right and a truck was directly to my left. To my right a truck was trying to merge real fast as if it didn't see me, but with a truck to my left and a car right behind me, there was nowhere to go / so I had to ride screaming on the yellow line in the middle of the two trucks so I wouldn't get squashed.

So after Nashville and Memphis, I actually started to have fun even though my throat felt like a wet nylon stocking from screaming so much, and my ass hurt because my pelvic bone was trying to cut its way through my ass to the bike seat. I'd made it through a couple of my worst cold-sweat nightmares and I was alive with a rash on my ass.

When I stopped to get gas I actually think I swaggered, although not on purpose. After sitting with your legs open against a two-hundred-mile-per-hour wind, you don't stand real tall.

I felt alive and alone in the best way. No one could intimidate me or give me shit because I had bug guts all over me and could keep a bike upright and pass a truck in the crosswinds with a war cry. I'd just been through traffic hell and now I was actually a biker who'd earned the right to spit on any road, even though I never did because I never practiced, because I knew it'd just drool down my chin inside the helmet.

The counter girls kind of smiled at me like I had gotten a doctorate. I imagined this is how guys must feel a lot of the time, but often they never did anything except stand there.

Once some RV lady said, "Wow, it must be pretty exhausting riding on the back of that thing." I just smiled and said "Yeah, I guess so," slipped my leather gloves back on and took off.

Finally... here was the actual living in *the here and now* that took the edge off my existential fear of time going on forever.

I started taking photographs of my bike like it was a new lover. Still, I never gave her a name because I just don't get into naming dependable toasters and stuff. I took pictures of the bike in front of a couple of disappointing-looking post offices, and I also took pictures of it in a herd of cattle with the sun setting in the background. The cows looked at my bike like it was a cow they wanted to understand and I felt peace. I took three rolls of film that would later come out blank because my camera was broken.

That's okay. I enjoy the act of taking pictures more than looking at pictures because it really gets me to slow down and really take note of what's around me, without counting on some wimpy photo later.

Yeah, no wimpy photos for me when I'm old and cranky. When all my retirement community neighbors have their lives entirely recorded on videotape, and laugh and laugh at the memories, I'll just rock back and forth wondering where I last set down my teeth, dammit. I'll be thinking that if I'd only had a photo album, I wouldn't always be in my slippers yelling at somebody's grandkids across the street.

Here and now./Now that I was actually enjoying myself, I started seeing other bikes. And that meant I could start checking out the social structure of other bikers on the road. Here's how it goes:

If you have a Harley, there ain't a damn thing wrong with you unless you're a blatant asshole. But even if you are an asshole, a Harley can be personality spackle in that it'll cover over any deficiencies. That's why balding midlife-crisis boys get them.

Sadly enough, Harleys are usually the bikes you see broken down on the side of the road. I think they're better for riding around your block and showing off like a mating bird, but I don't know how far I'd wanna go. A whole lotta myth, and not known for being reliable. But you won't have to tap on people's shoulders and tell them how cool you are, because a Harley will do it for you. Once you get a Harley, you don't even need a relationship.

I want one so bad, my nipples sting just thinking about it.

If you get a Japanese bike, you'd better have one hell of a sense of humor or just stay at home. If you're a girl, they say you can ride just about anything and it's okay. But they're dependable and you can go far if you've got to get out of town fast because you've bought foreign.

I'm not much for breaking in with the crotch-rocket set. These are mostly hyper white suburban guys who like shiny red plastic things. In their teens and twenties, they still go around with Oxy wash in their pockets to look like they're glad to see you, pretending they're in a superhero comic book world. But stereotypes often ring hollow and when you come face to face with one of these guys they end up being okay, so never mind.

I want acceptance from the slow-riding Harley set because they have a certain kind of panache. The men get big and hairy, and even the faded rose tattoo Harley chicks with their flat tits don't fear getting leather faces in the sun.

In Arkansas, I was trying to catch up to these two guys on Harleys way up ahead in the distance. I caught up to them, and they had their beat-up old leathers on and bandannas on their heads. I'm telling you, I felt cool just riding behind them on the cracked yellow highway. But they ignored me/and now that I was a real live biker, *I demanded notice.*

Like a good dog introducing herself in the park, I sped up, passed them, and pulled in front of the first guy to show him my American-girl thighs and New Jersey tags. I let them sniff my ass in the park for a minute, then they pulled back out to pass me, and when they did they waved and nodded as they took their places back in front of me. I knew the Kawasaki thing was forgiven because I was a girl and they'd let me ride with them. Six paces behind, but that's okay: They were my highway emissaries.

Chapter Thirty-One
I'M DETERMINED TO ONE DAY UNDERSTAND AND LOVE ANAL SEX BECAUSE I'M CONVINCED I MUST BE MISSING SOMETHING

Oklahoma was beautiful, not only because it was flat and yellow, but because it meant I was actually out West. I'd totally stopped feeling two inches tall as I was going through the Ozarks in Arkansas. But Oklahoma welcomed me by smacking me over at a constant forty-five degree angle with the fucking crosswinds.

Fuck thinking about brand-new folk songs. I sang the national anthem through my teeth for half a day until I could ride upright again.

In Oklahoma, I continued to get the same kind of doctoral respect from the girls behind the counters at gas stations, and if there was a guy behind the counter, he usually did a lot of relaxed leaning against the register or smoothie machine. I'd half expect him to challenge me to see how high I could pee, and he'd have that half-lidded look that was supposed to appear like he'd just finished having sex / why? / Because studs have always just had sex. And me walking in with D-cups, splattered bug guts on my jacket, and swaggering like the tired cheerleader because of the rash on my ass, was just too much of a challenge for a virile guy working in a store with primary color soda signs.

It got so I counted on at least three different people commenting in some way whenever I stopped for gas. I wanted to see other women riding so I'd feel less like a freak, but I only ran into girls who rode on back. They never really waved or gave me cool directions. They just smiled exactly as much as their boyfriends or husbands did.

So anyway, now in Oklahoma, I was bonding with this truckdriver who was filling up the tanks at a gas station about riding motorcycles and how much KOA ("Kampgrounds of America") campgrounds sucked. Sometimes you could actually see a tacky KOA from a major highway. Besides, any place that figured it was clever to spell things with Ks instead of Cs, was pathetic. It was getting kind of late to ride on, and he told me about some winding back roads and a decent campground a half-hour away. / Cool. / We were swapping stories in deep voices.

The winding ride to the campground wasn't so bad because there weren't any cars on the road. Curves really were fun, but I still wanted to take a motorcycle-riding course when I got home because my stomach still chewed on itself doing curves high up on the edges of mountains. I've seen those Harley guys swinging into curves happy like an Olivia Newton-John song, and that's what I wanted.

It started to drizzle when I got about five minutes from the campground.

When I got there, the camp office was closed and I was happy. I wasn't gonna be honest and pay if I didn't have to. These campsites were 10 bucks, and that still seemed steep to me for just sleeping outside and peeing in the dirt and covering it over like a cat. I rode around and they weren't so bad, but at the end of the road I saw a sign for sites available for people with horse trailers at 7 bucks. Three dollars saved. For 3 bucks I could buy more bread and cheese or a book of postcard stamps.

I figured I might actually have to pay if someone was gonna ride around in the morning collecting money, so I rode on up the muddy hill to the $7 horse campgrounds.

There was a bald spot at the top of the hill, with about five empty sites around a little circular drive. I looked around for a spot under some trees around the edge, but underneath them there were some greasy, uneven picnic tables, mounds of horse shit, leftover hay, and deep tire grooves filling up with rain.

I saw an opening through a cluster of trees behind one of the sites, and I figured there might be a little trail down the other side of the hill, so I slowly pushed my bike through some mud and horse shit. It took me fifteen minutes of getting stuck in mud and rocking my bike back and forth to get through one horse campsite. There was a hiking trail, and it was wide enough for my bike so I wound down through some trees and I figured I'd find a nice little private place just a few yards down.

Maybe I could actually have some privacy and masturbate tonight and not see myself in court going "You're right. It's all my fault. Yeah, I guess I was raped because he heard me masturbating alone in my tent."

I was excited and felt like I was on an adventure as I started rolling my fully loaded bike down the trail of wet leaves. Until you enter a soggy trail in a thick clump of trees, you don't realize how much light there is in an open sky just before dark. No problem: I switched on my little headlight and slowly continued down through the trees. I might as well have been holding up a lighter and singing "la la la" as I saw my front tire aim for a big shiny flat rock. In slow motion, Snowballus in my head screamed, "NO: wet leaves and slippery rocks—NOT GOOD." and by the time I turned my handlebars to miss the rock I was already *on* the rock, so the fully loaded bike wiped out and fell on my leg, leaving me with some more wife-beater bruises that later got hard like peach pits.

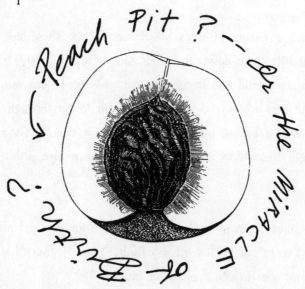

Peach Pit ? — Or the MiRACLE of Birth?

I sat up with my leg still under the bike and wiped my hands on my stomach.

So far, every time I've fallen on my bike, I've realized it's not all fire and brimstone./So far./Of course I haven't wiped out at over 10 mph./So far.

I quickly turned off the key in the ignition and pulled myself out from under the bike. I tried to lift the bike back up, but I was facing downhill and my boots kept losing traction in the mud. In the midst of these trees I could barely see outlines. I looked up at the dark blue sky through the tops of the black trees and waited for my eyes to adjust.

I looked around me and only saw black./I heard sounds like a faraway river, but I knew they were leaves blowing in the sky. For a tea bag moment, everything was as it was supposed to be. I breathed with the trees and felt separated from the collective human consciousness: I didn't want to conquer anything, didn't want to build cheap aluminum developments or shopping centers. I felt I belonged and would've asked for permission to stay if I'd known how. Natural, no running motors, no complaints, or pink hairbrushes. These unplanned moments of actually feeling like a natural part of the planet, like a human being who eats alfalfa sprouts and doesn't float on top of the earth like an oil slick, are so few and too far between.

This sound of gasoline spilling out of my tank politely tapped on the gray matter of my brain and asked for the next dance. . .

. . . it was enough to spew me back onto the unwaxed linoleum floor of my mind and make me go "oh, fuck!" I imagined myself starting my bike and blowing up in flames. Weeks later a couple of park rangers out for a quiet, unheterosexual fuck in the woods would've found me, my bike, and all my things, charred to a hollow crisp. They would've been able to fit everything in a little Ziploc sandwich bag and hand it to my mom.

That thought gave me the strength of a man-hating feminist who's just seen a man pee in public, so I grabbed hold of the silver handlebars along with the back of the seat and pushed so hard that I popped out my future children. The bike slid across the path, and I even turned it in a circle like clock hands. But

it wasn't until I lost all vanity and screamed deep down back from New Jersey, that I could lift the bike up.

My legs shook and my heart was running around me in circles beating tom-toms, chanting for me to join the YMCA as soon as I got home. I pushed my gear back into place so I could balance the bike. I felt for the kickstand with my foot, but thought I might pass out, so I draped my body over the seat to bring blood to my head.

About a half hour later I caught my breath and figured any gas that'd leaked had evaporated by now, but the bike wouldn't start. I was relaxed as I looked the bike over and plugged in some little unplugged thing near the clutch and the headlight went back on and the bike started right up when I turned the key. I swung my leg over the seat, and slowly rode the bike back up the path, staying up with my feet.

Ahead in the headlight's beam I saw a darling little frog hopping across the path and wondered how many of the poor little creatures I'd unknowingly murdered riding down into my herbal tea experience and how many more critters I was tied to karmically.

I feel guilty
about pouring
salt on all those
slugs...
I can still hear
their SCREAMS in my
sleep.

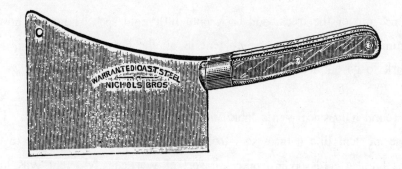

But not fleas. I "love" smashing their little crunchy bodies and I'll probably rot in hell for it. And hell is probably some giant flea crushing <u>me</u> between his hairy knees over and over... forever... like some kind of Prometheus-thing.

Once out of the trees, and back onto little bald spot, I noticed how hard it was raining. I couldn't set up my tent in all the horse shit and mud, and it was too dark to go out looking for a $10 campsite.

I found a lopsided picnic table with a few little trees around it. I decided to use my tent like a tarp, so I took a few corners and tied them to the trees with the bungee cords on my bike. It sort of worked. My tent was long, narrow, and had a lot of different weather flaps, so it looked like a huge floppy fabric labia hanging over a greasy picnic table. I finally used my rain gear for the first time when I took it out of my saddlebag and spread it on the table.

I pulled out my sleeping bag and laid it over the rain gear, stripped out of my muddy clothes, and crawled inside where it was cozy. As long as there was no breeze, and I lay on the table diagonally with my knees bent, I could stay pretty dry. I felt so competent, I totally fell in love with myself. That night I slept real well, and didn't even open my eyes in the middle of the night when a car pulled up to the site next to me. Full of peace and still in love with myself, I listened as a guy and his little kid set up their tent in front of the headlights of their car, and when I finally heard them shut the car off and zip up the door of the tent behind them, I fell back to sleep.

CHAPTER THIRTY-TWO
Living UNDER a Full Bladder and Calling it a Jersey Tent

"Is that how you put tents up in New Jersey?"

I woke up on the picnic table to a man's Texas accent somewhere behind me. "Huh?" I barely focused on a bear of a guy in jeans and an undershirt with long curly gray hair and a beard that went down to his potbelly. He was putting wood on a fire, and he had a lot of faded tattoos on his gritty arms. "Oh, hi. Yeah, New Jersey." I smoothed down my hair and looked around.

He'd seen the tags on my bike. It wasn't raining anymore and my tent was hanging about six inches above my stomach, bloated with water. I carefully turned over in my sleeping bag onto my stomach and reached down on the bench for my glasses.

I started to push myself out of my bag until I realized I wasn't wearing anything. He politely turned around and put a pot down near the fire. "Want some coffee?"

I put on my wet clothes, and we had some gourmet vanilla-flavored coffee that was so sweet it didn't even need sugar. His little boy came skipping back from the bathrooms with a toothbrush and a towel in his hand, and we had some pancakes and sausage. His name was Ole—pronounced like the margarine— and his little boy's name was Rory. Ole was going from Texas to Alabama to see his daughter who was thirty and dying of ovarian cancer. Her mother was dying from something too, but I don't remember what. He just kind of shrugged his shoulders and rubbed his little kid on the back and asked me if I wanted more sausage.

When we were done I dumped all the water off my tent and packed up my bike. I got on my bike and started walk-riding it to a flatter part of the hill's bald spot and I held out my hand to shake theirs, but they both came over and gave me hugs.

Ole handed me a white business card covered in layers of brown fingerprints that read "1-800-PUNISH U" in the middle. In the lower right-hand corner, the name "MARK" was printed in tiny capital letters. Ole said some old friends of his had a double-wide trailer home bed and breakfast in Amarillo. He said it was nothing fancy, but tell them he sent me and they'd probably give me a break.

"What's 1-800-PUNISH U?" I asked.

Ole explained that Bark Flammers and his lesbian wife, Kris Kovique, had a call-in revenge business. Like if your man done you wrong, you can call 1-800-PUNISH U, and have a tall, strapping woman hired to follow him around, yell obscenities at him all day, then throw tantrums when he's in public with the new woman. A perfect service for anyone who's way too busy to stalk or get revenge, Ole said.

"What a fantastic idea," I said. "It's the kind of business idea whose time has come."

"They even do car damage," Ole said. But you had to ask for it by code, and it cost extra.

I was into looking these people up even though I usually hated bed and breakfasts. I didn't like to be that close to strangers who were pretending to be charming and nice in a cute Victorian way, but I didn't think I'd have to be worried about that with these folks.

The last place I went to was the Inn at Penn Cove with my mother, on Whidbey Island up in Washington State. When I asked the little husband guy who ran the place with his little jumpy wife, where they were from, he said with a liver-lipped smile, "Spiritually or geographically?" I turned my head because I just had to roll my eyes.

When the little man finally admitted he was from Manhattan with another shaky smile, I figured he'd been beaten out of town because he was so spinelessly creepy. I could see him saying to his wife they could buy a nice bed and breakfast and be simple loving people in the country./L.L. Bean warm and cozy fantasies have cost people a lot of money and left people with a lot of nonreturnable merchandise, in spite of an exceptional guarantee policy.

I guess he didn't figure on having to smile so much or changing the sheets every night. But at $225 a night, exceptional service really is what it's all about for me, and when he didn't change the sheets the second night, I bled the first night of my period all over his king-size Victorian rose prints.

La La La.

I thanked Ole for the tip on the place to stay and waved good-bye. He said to call them first. I took off gently because after last night I was afraid I'd even wipe out on cracker-dry hard-top, and there'd be nothing more embarrassing than falling over as people watched you ride away in a black leather jacket with FLAM on the back.

The Texas Panhandle totally sucked. The air was hot, dusty, and dry and even the sagebrush was too tired to roll/it was like riding forever on someone's hot yellow kitchen counter while their house was on fire. The most exciting things were the concrete pimples and gashes in the middle of my lane. How did *New Jersey* get such a bad reputation? I swear, ever since I passed the welcome-to-Texas sign, my nose got stuffed up and started running. Eventually I got off 40 and started riding on 66 so I could at least busy myself with romantic thoughts of all the famous people who'd ridden the same road. A few other Route 66 Guide Book people were there too, smiling like the word "cheese."

It was perfect that just about the time my arms started to look like beef jerky from the sun, I was close to the Amarillo exit. I pulled into the nearest gas station and I suddenly had to pee so bad. I didn't notice that I flipped the kickstand down with the tip of my boot into a soft patch of sand. I was getting so good at jumping off a falling bike. I didn't care how much gas was leaking out of my bike as I ran to the bathroom.

I came back out, lifted up my bike, and went inside one of my bags for a cheese sandwich. There's usually nothing better than a good sourdough and the kind of cheese so sharp, your face caves in, but I'd ended up with some kind of Texas Road Fondue: The cheese in my reused plastic bags had ended up crumbly orange balls swimming in clear orange oil, and the bread ended up mashed flat from the bungee cords on my bike. Mmm Mmm good.

I called the 1-800 number and a man's cheerful voice answered, "Jell-O!"

Chapter Thirty-Four
Untitled

Bark gave me directions to their trailer. He said it was in the back part of a McDonald's drive-thru. Then I called to check back in with Hodie and she said my dad had just died, so I decided to slow down.

chapter thirty-five
The Rogaine Warrior and the Homeless Golfer

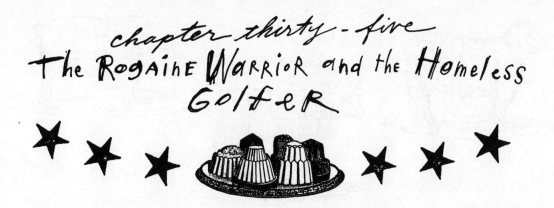

A funny couple, these two were. Kris Kovique was a French lesbian who'd married Bark Flammers, a gay man who liked straight guys, so she could stay in the country. They had six or seven yellow Labs barking and bouncing all over the place when I drove up to the house.

I pulled the sweaty fabric of my jeans from my skin and looked up. The sun was setting behind the dry cleaners across the street, and the striated clouds covered the purple sky like the stretch marks on my hips.

Bark and Kris came outside with big smiles on their faces and cigars in their mouths. Kris dressed in a relaxed preppy way, like a homeless golfer, and Bark dressed in loose oatmeal linen like a magazine ad.

I said hello and that they had a lot of dogs. Bark said if we were in Korea their place would probably be called a yellow meat dog farm because they eat big yellow meat dogs.

Kris said they once lived next to a Korean church and got nervous about the dogs, so she went over to introduce them. She said for them to look at their eyes, pet them, get to know them, they were good dogs and had tags and all. They laughed and told her to relax, that they didn't just go hunting for dogs on the street. She asked what dogs tasted like./They said like cats.

I unpacked my bags and Bark took me for a ride around Amarillo in his foofy Lexus. When it came out that we both had birthdays on August tenth, we stopped being so polite and started talking like stripped-down pigs.

Bark said if Texas was a great big made-up whore, Amarillo would be the underside of her breast. The sweaty fold of a large breast.

He waved over at my chest. "You've got great big breasts. You know what it's like under there when it's hot."

"Yeah, but they don't get like that. I bet you your testicles get a whole lot sweatier than the underside of a couple D-cups."

"Yes." he raised his eyebrows and nodded at the road. "I could tell you all about testicles."

"Well, they get pretty sweaty."

"Yes, yes they do, but we have that *special skin*. Testicles can be long one minute, short the next. They contract. Your breasts can't do that."

He had me there.

"I'll be turning forty this August," he said. "And the way I see it, forty is a great big passport to 'I don't care.'" He said that he would eat lemon meringue pie every day if he wanted because lemon meringue pie made him think clearly. He said there was never enough. He would become agoraphobic and have it delivered, and wear his shorts up to his chest when he answered the door.

"Sure, I eat lemon meringue pie every day now, but I dance around while I eat it so I'll burn calories at the same time. Two birds at one time, like sex in the shower," he said. "But when I'm forty I won't care about anything except my 401(k) plan. I won't even care that Kris calls me the Rogaine warrior in public."

He said he thought about God more, now that he was closer to dying. He asked, "What if God were really gay and in the end we were judged on our hair and how good our blow jobs were? And what about those who never gave a blow job? Would they have just one chance to fellate for their soul?"

I just looked out the window and said I agreed with the sweaty fold thing.

He asked me if I were straight or gay, and I kind of said I thought I was both, but I wasn't totally sure because although I liked girl/girl porn made by straight guys, I'd never actually been with a woman.

"Look, I've been with lots of women, and I can tell you, foreplay with women is like a goddamn minefield. I mean, you've gotta first find this little tiny *thing*, and carefully pull everything back to *reveal* it. All these little tiny folds for one little *thing*. But penises." Bark slapped his thighs. "I mean, no matter how small they are, they're right *there*, and God!—You can yank it, pull it, throw things at it. You don't have to be careful."

"You're right, men are easy." I agreed. The guys I'd been with thought a woman was wild in bed if she moved.

"Hey, how would you like to come work for me as a stalker?" Bark asked me. "You could be labeled The Mad Latina Stalker. You can make an easy hundred bucks a day following some guy around, shrieking at him, and writing all over his car with lipstick."

"You're kidding." I laughed.

"No, no, no. I've got all sorts of package deals. I've got Mild Stalking packages, those are only half-days of harrassment; I've got less expensive crank call packages—"

"No thanks. Sounds great, but stopping here now would be like swimming a lap halfway." I rolled myself a cigarette like some old pioneer guy with a lot of dreams. "Yep." I sighed. "If California doesn't pan out for me, I'll come back."

We drove around a little more. We stopped for some nonfat frozen yogurt, and he ordered a nonfat de-caf latte. When we got back to the trailer, the sky was indigo blue, and we sat around a fire in the grill, smoked cigarettes, and drank Kris's homemade plum wine.

CHAPTER THIRTY-SIX
Hubba Hubba, Bring on the Dancing Girls

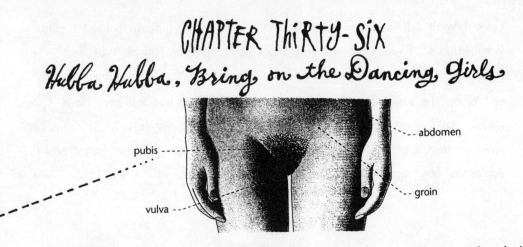

pubis - - - - -
abdomen - - - -
vulva - - - -
groin - - - -

I woke up to a pale yellow sky on the hard foam trailer sofa-thing, with a bad wine hangover. So I drank about a gallon of water and left twenty dollars along with my cheap Xeroxed calling card under the salt and pepper shakers on the kitchen table.

Hangovers make me filthy, sexy, and easygoing like a dried-out tropical cocktail./Like I had a good time not on my own. And on my own bike, at something like 6 A.M. with a Texas yellow sky. I felt crusty and beautifully wrinkled, unwashed, and sweaty.

I threw my leg over and sat on my bike's smiling face.

And thank God I haven't been wearing pantyhose, huh? Pantyhose used to be sexy until I started thinking about going down on women. Then pantyhose became sweat trappers that made people get yeast infections, and yeast infections are not sexy even though your legs may look good at the same time.

215

Once I went into a public office bathroom after a big lady in polyester pants was finished. Even after she pulled her pants back up, which was like resealing a Ziploc bag, it smelled like a trapped and fearful vagina in there, and when she walked out, I wanted to run after her and tell her, *Hey!—yeah, you. . . set your vagina free. Wear cotton. Open your legs/laugh/lean back on your desk and let the wind rush between your legs like an unrestrained adolescent boy, and you will smell so good everybody will want to go down on you.*

Just you watch.

But instead I said nothing and felt sad for her *chocha*. Polyester pants and nylons are like tying your pussy to a piano and beating the poor little thing with wire hangers./Oh. The schizophrenic stories it could tell if it grew up and wrote a book.

Whether you're a man or a woman, lots of water is good.

Especially when you've been *with* a man. That is the worst smell in the world. And they call *us* fish? I don't think so, rotting squid boy. After you, I want to leave my own body and skip through some herbal pasture in the Swiss Alps until I smell like fennel. Sure, coming inside and outside, just squirting things from every orifice like a pimple is great, but I advocate the use of condoms simply for smelling more like something that doesn't make the dogs retch quite so much.

It took me a long time to get used to sucking on men I hardly knew (most of the men I'd been with, I hardly knew). Actually, the sucking wasn't so bad, it was the swallowing. When I was ten, I read in a porn advice column that it was like abandoning the ship if you didn't. So I did. It was quite a few years before I started bringing a bottle of fresh orange juice next to the bed.

Once when I was eighteen or nineteen, and going down on this married Vietnam vet truckdriver with a southern accent, I pulled the tip of his penis out of my mouth, looked up at him, me being cute and young with a ponytail on the top of my head, and I asked, "What's this?" I ran the tip of my tongue under a little scar I felt under his penis. He said, "Well, baby doll," because he called me baby doll a lot, "you get pretty sweaty when you sit in a truck all day, and well, I got warts. But it's okay now because they all got cut off."

I pretended I heard the phone ring in the other room and got up because whoring around isn't nearly as fun and glamorous as it looks.

I look back and think I would've felt better about a lot of these old sepia-toned blow jobs if I'd gotten some money. It isn't so smart doing all your favors for free.

BUT BacK TO VaGINAS.

I remember back when I was in some art class in my first or second year of school. I'd always preferred drawing women's bodies because they were just

217

more beautiful somehow. They never looked like they were just standing there, being paid 7 bucks an hour to be drawn, unlike the men, who looked like they were waiting for a cavity search.

And then this dark-haired lady rushed in late to the studio wearing a double-breasted leopard print fake fur coat. We were all stinky, pretentious art geeks waiting around in front of the newsprint pads on our easels, hands on our hips, sweaty conte crayons in our fists.

She unapologetically blew in smelling of the real live outside world, and without catching anyone's eyes, she kicked her thick high heels off against the wall, unbuttoned her coat, and threw it on a paint-splattered chair as if we were just mosquitoes. She had beautiful round hips like she'd swallowed a giant coffee cup, and a triangle of pubic hair six inches in front like static electricity. It could've easily been compared to Bette Midler's stage presence./ But more accessible at 7 bucks an hour.

I never saw anything more beautiful. She was living her life letting the wind fly through her crotch like that little overeager adolescent boy, and I could almost imagine her walking through the city free and easy, wearing that leopard coat with her legs open and in the air.

And for the next three hours all I could do is stare, and I wanted to go up and bury my face between her legs for the afternoon. I wouldn't have known what to do once I was there—maybe I would've sung muffled songs—but that was okay.

Three hours of fluffy black triangles on my newsprint. I needed an excuse to just stare. And as the teacher walked around the class to give tips and help us out, he quickly bypassed me to help other students.

When our three hours were up, she jumped off the modeling platform and buttoned her coat on her way out the front door.

After that, I didn't give heterosexual men such a hard time anymore about spontaneously shouting things like "Hubba hubba! Bring on the dancing girls!"

I understand your pain, brother man.

I'd suppressed a whole series of snorting noises for three hours, and it was even harder than replacing the alternater in my VW Bug or graduating college. Like Jim Morrison, I'd broken on through to the other side, and once you even consider crossing over, you never quite look at Dolly Parton the same way.

Sure, hard-ons on the living room sofa are magnificent—sex is sex. Even two dogs fucking in front of a sunset can be erotic, depending on how you film it, but now I want more than a few extra fucking positions and morning words of affection. I want fingers, teeth, knees, laughter, time, and a whole lot of magic that means not talking things to a bloody pulp.

I just couldn't keep my hands off myself, so I masturbated all winter until I met a nice boy in the spring I could practice lesbian sex with.

Jeff was his name, and I met him in the middle of one of those tiny Philadelphia alleys. I imagine if he hasn't admitted he's gay yet, he probably will one day. Jeff was riding a skateboard and carrying a laundry basket of clothes. He stopped, blew his cowlick out of his face, and smiled at me.

I ended up going over to his little trinity apartment for dinner. A trinity is usually a building over a hundred years old, with three floors, one room on top of another, with very tiny staircases so narrow and windy, most people have to push their mattresses through windows upstairs. There was a little fireplace on every floor, and he set up a table in front of the first-floor fireplace and served me a multicourse gourmet meal.

I waited probably a week and a half to have sex with him. By then, I felt I knew him well enough to show him a lesbian sex book, so I gave it to him to take home and study. The next night, he came back to my apartment with a gourmet hard-on and quickly fed me another dinner.

Then he tried to fist me just like how the book said.

We didn't count on the fact that it might be a lot harder because he was a guy, more specifically a ceramicist with large hands, and I'd never even had anything larger in me than a hand carved rubber dildo named Big Bob.

Night after night he fed me rich gourmet food and red wine, and tried to fit his whole hand inside me afterward in front of the fireplace. It felt great enough for me to almost pass out, but I soon got bored with trying so hard to make it up past that one knuckle.

I'd be in my own world, floating like a cherub, nerve endings flying behind me like streamers, my muscles pulling off my bones, and singing happy opera songs. . . he'd push his hand up just a little farther, all squishy with lube and I'd gasp, "Okay, wait," . . . but he'd try and do one last little push to pop his thumb past—man, my cunt closed down hard like a garbage truck and it'd be over.

Then he'd ask me if he could fuck me up the ass yet and I'd laugh.

"No, but I'll tell you what."

"What?"

"I'll go down on you."

"Oh, okay."

221

"Just lean back a little. . . there you go. Now unzip your pants. . . pull the front down a little. Okay, good. Here, take the hairbrush and brush my hair while I do this."

And this was the first time since I'd made the conscious decision not to swallow that I didn't swallow when he came. It landed on his stomach, and I leaned in to look closer.

It'd always seemed too laced with potent power to let a blob just lie there on a stomach doing nothing. It wasn't impregnating anything, landing on someone's face, or waiting like Vincent Price in the reservoir tip of a condom like "Ha ha ha! I'm gonna get you, fucker!" / My job was to dance around semen like a voodoo bonfire, but this was a letdown. Little bubbles and tiny string blobs that looked like they came from raw eggs sat there on his stomach and I knew then that I would never swallow again, no matter if I loved a guy enough to let him perform surgery on me or see my tits sag to either side of my chest when I lay down.

Sometimes fathers *are* blobs of semen, and if you're still waiting for them to bounce you on their knees, it's time to move on.

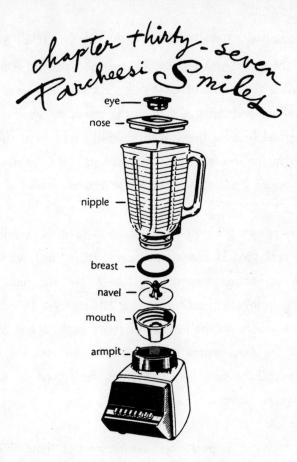

eye —
nose —
nipple —
breast —
navel —
mouth —
armpit —

I finally rode off the last bit of dusty road and onto the strip of blacktop that would take me to I-40. I realized I hadn't even decided how far I was going or where I was going. But between the hangover, the morning, the bike, and the fact that I was already more than half way across America, I was feeling pretty good about everything / Even my own semen daddy-o.

On fiftieth thought, he wasn't really such a jerk. He'd marched a whole lot for civil rights back in the sixties—that's how he and my mom met—and once in awhile I'll be watching some kind of civil rights documentary on PBS, and catch a glimpse of him smiling or holding a sign in the corner of some photo. It makes me kind of proud because that's who he really is. I even caught a glimpse of him once in the movie *Alice's Restaurant*. He's the friendly looking guy wearing horn-rimmed glasses, standing in the church pews.

I think that people who are geniuses or supposed to save the world, well, they're not usually real good at one-on-one family-stuff and we've got to cut them some slack for it, because somebody's got to go out and make good movies, write poetry, paint paintings, or make sure we get the right to vote, get a good education, and sit anywhere on the bus on the way back to our decent housing. Some of us are just too damn scared to rock the boat and ask the waiter for a bowl of soup without all the flies. "Ah, hell it's damn good for us," we say, and we even tip twenty percent.

So we really need to write a thank-you note to some of these folks, because for a lot of them, the whiny kid-thing was just a mistake that sounded good at the time. / Nothing like carrying an egg around for a week without breaking it. Decades and decades of need, resentment, and blame.

chapter Thirty-Eight
Out of The Closet and Into the Laps of Dogs

I didn't get to actually masturbate until I got to Flagstaff, Arizona.

A couple of my friends, Gina and Sadie, were on vacation and offered to let me take a break and watch the dogs while they were gone.

I know I talk about sex a lot, but it's only because I'm fondly remembering my sex drive as if it were something in a scrapbook. Sure, I may be young and fertile like cow manure, but these days I've got the sex drive of an old encyclopedia. I spent all my pennies in a candy store one afternoon, and there's absolutely nothing left. I don't care what they say about energy being replenished and stuff. Yeah, let's see them turn a raisin back into a fresh potato. Now instead of coming home every night, lighting candles, and having multiple orgasms by myself until 5 A.M., I just pop in a gay boy porn tape once a month and blow my chakras in less than five minutes. I've swept up cat litter with more gusto. That's what hurts.

I want to fondly remember my sex drive like misty water colored memories of the way we were.

Except a woman once told me that most people don't have sex to have sex. Almost always, she said, there ends up being a different reason. Like feeling power or need/or powerfully needy.

I have a friend who only swallowed because she didn't want the sheets to get messy. That this was her only option for clean sheets pissed her off so much she became a lesbian. But now her life is full of bitchy women who tell her what's wrong with everything from her inner soul down to the way she wakes up in the morning.

This is not an example of sex for deeper reasons, but doing things *during* sex for deeper reasons.

At this point, now that sex for the wrong reasons—or any reason, for that matter—is out of the way for me, I've learned that my most perfect Zen lover would sit quietly reading tabloid magazines all evening while I get cartoons done in front of the TV, and when I ask what they're thinking, they look over at me and say:

"Nothing."

★

So anyway, back in Arizona, my friends left the house key in the mailbox and as soon as I opened the door, three big dogs stood in the hallway barking at me for a very long time.

By midnight, I finally refused to let anything stand in my way of a shower and a real bed, so I stopped trying to feed my mustard and sugar packets to them and talking baby talk.

Out of desperation, I finally decided to be rough, so I played alpha dog again: I loudly spit for them all to go and sit down. I thought there'd be some arguing, but they shut up and retreated to the kitchen.

I dropped all my clothes on the floor, shuffled straight to the shower, and noticed Gina and Sadie had a hand-held shower massage.

And just as I started to come, the doorbell rang.

La la la.

chapter thirty-nine
Disco Inferno

It was a sweet gray-haired neighbor lady who'd wondered who I was because they'd heard the dogs barking earlier. I told them my friends were gone for ten days or so and that I was gonna house sit while they were gone.

The next day I lay out in their backyard with my shirt off so I'd even out my tan. The tan line from my wristwatch was amazing. It was a proud tan. A lot of people are proud of their tans as if they actually went to school or studied for one, but I was proud of my watchband tan line because it meant I'd really ridden a true live motorcycle outside. Across America.

Some guy named Bob came over and he was a friend of Gina and Sadie's. They wanted him to come by and check on the dogs in case I got hit by a truck and didn't make it over.

He found a note on the refrigerator about how much to feed the dogs and to not let the buff cat outside. Ever. Bob and I wondered if buff in this case meant a color, a strong cat, or a naked cat. We called the number on the note, and they said "color."

One of the dogs kept leaving skid marks on the carpeting, and by the end of the week they looked like the stretch marks in the Texas sky.

Bob came over a lot, and we laughed at our own jokes until our faces and stomachs hurt. Laughing with him would've been sexy if he weren't so thin and neurotic. The Woody Allen types never did it for me. If you ask guys like this what they're thinking, the list could be painfully endless.

As the second week started, Bob was afraid we hadn't taken good enough care of the house, and he started reverting back to some sort of childhood panic about the whole thing. He started sweating. And then he ran around watering the plants and scrubbing the skid marks off the carpeting.

Then he got pissed off because he was afraid of Gina and Sadie, so he made jokes about us leaving crumbs in their bed, spilling mayonnaise in their practical underwear drawer, and taking Polaroids of himself wearing their clothes.

Before they came home I just made sure I picked out all the pubic hairs stuck in the shower massage.

So that was about it for Arizona.

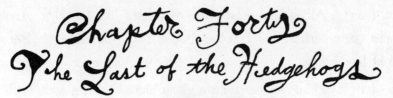

Chapter Forty
The Last of the Hedgehogs

KINGMAN, ARIZONA
(like "king me!" checkers with my sister)

NEEDLES, CALIFORNIA
(it's not weather, it's chemotherapy . . .)

BARSTOW
(. . . and hotter than a whore in love)

THE MOJAVE DESERT
(huh?)

I got lost for the first time after passing through the Mojave Desert, and found myself on a road heading south to Palm Springs. I thought of old ladies with cotton-white buns in their hair, rocking in chairs, so I stopped at a little tiny gas station/store-thing for directions. Not a fluorescent light or mass-produced sign to be found. All around outside looked wasted like the U.S. Army had tested bombs years earlier, and I looked around for deformed pigs. But this store looked like a bag lady because, as I later learned, everyone who simply stopped by left something—a hat with a photo pinned to it, a sock with a note on it, a rusty pot with a signature on it, and whatever—these things would be hung outside the store on the porch, around the windows, from the awnings, tacked to the wall, or nailed on the walls inside.

I was hot, tired, and pissed about getting lost and losing so much time in the desert. So I was in a bad mood as I pulled in front and unsnapped my map from the gas tank to ask for directions inside.

I walked up to the counter, smiled and asked something about how to get out of there.

I ended up chatting with the guy behind the counter for a while. He talked about all the old astronauts who used to go to some bar that used to be down the road. I really didn't care, because those guys cut their hair too short, and white guys with really short hair scare me.

Then this guy, about thirty-five years old, came in wearing a beat-up cowboy hat. He'd been sunburned so long, his skin was all little bumpy dots, and he was wearing real faded blue jeans—not the kind you *buy* faded. You can tell, no matter how old they are because there are still remembers of blue at the seams, in the creases and around the pockets.

He came in, took off his hat, combed his fingers through his dusty blond hair, nodded at me, and smiled. I smiled back nervously and accidentally looked down at his brass "Arizona" belt buckle because I couldn't look at his face too long. The buckle was an oval shape and every "Arizona" letter had been cut out and glued on top. I suddenly realized it probably looked like I was staring at his crotch, so without the finesse I would've hoped for, I yanked my gaze up to the ceiling, where there were dozens of posters of blond girls in blue bikinis, squeezing bottles of beer and motor oil between their airbrushed tits.

Sex, sex, sex was everywhere and I was just trying to get directions home without losing my virginity or anyone else's. No wonder Fundamentalists try to cram their genitals back up into their pelvic cavities. How can one expect to stay faithful to one's wife and steer clear of blow jobs and sodomy when you even find sex is spraying like a geyser from a gas station in the desert?

"Come on back and I'll tell you about what I'm doing. You'll probably think it's really cool. I'm going on the Pacific Coast Trail in a cart pulled by a horse and a donkey," the man in the Arizona belt buckle said with a huge white grin. My hair was flat, bugs were splattered on my neck, and I had enough dirt on my face to bury my feelings, but I was surprised he looked at me with respect and desire: like I was some guy he wanted to date.

We went out to the back of the store, where his animals were in a little pen next to a little trailer. He was staying with the store owner in the trailer, sleeping on one of those hard foam sofa bench-things. There are so many

233

different kinds of sofas that convert into things like beds. TV tables, and kitchen counters, it's hard sometimes to simply say "sofa." Sofas have really evolved and are constantly redefining themselves like Madonna.

The man in the Arizona belt buckle and I talked and drank a beer even though it was eleven in the morning and by the time he popped open a second can of warm beer, he'd already asked me to go to the Pacific Coast Trail on his donkey cart with him. I laughed like *ha ha, that's really funny*, but I really started thinking about it. When would I ever get a chance like this to ride on a donkey and a cart up the Pacific coast? Someone said I could leave my bike behind the store, and I started to nod my head. I didn't really have to be back for any reason. He said it's real slow-going though. Like two miles an hour. I didn't care.

I was seriously tempted to hang out some more and get to know this guy, but then he made the mistake of going into graphic detail about a shit he took near a tractor one night while holding onto the horse's reins and clutching a big wad of toilet paper.

Again: *Graphic detail is fine as long as you don't say it out loud.*

I thought about how hard it is to get really, *really* clean on the road, and how he'd probably end up wanting me to rim him or something. When you're as oral as I am, you have big hips and think of things like that.

I wouldn't have been able to rise to that kind of occasion, so I said thanks for the offer and that I had to go. I took off real fast so I'd look cool and when I turned the corner I thanked God I didn't wipe out for once and look like an ass. I love leaving people. The more dramatically I leave them, the better. It is so much nicer than being left. Hopefully I will die first.

BAKERSFIELD
(Didn't they film a women's prison TV movie here starring a Charlie's Angel?)

LOST HILLS
("I am woman, hear me roar, something's too difficult for me to ignore. . . ")

COALINGUA
("One less bell to answer/One less egg to fry. . . ")

SALINA
(I-5 north: boring, dry, dusty, flat, except for thoughts of cunnilingus ever since Coalingua)

I looked at the mountains, smelled the California spices in the air, and loved the brown of my arms. No one was on the road and all I could hear was the rush of wind in my ears.

I felt alone and I loved America, but I didn't need to sing the national anthem and I was all right./I'd done it. I'd really, really done it. I'd made it and I felt the peace of living in the here and now and not worrying about where I'd be tomorrow or in fifty years.

CHAPTER FORTY-ONE
Laughing and Laughing Like It's the End of Your Own TV Show

This was it.

I'd made it.

Did I feel like a different woman?

No. I felt the same way right after I lost my virginity./I figured and hoped the insights and profound sense of accomplishment would hit me later along with the insights from that dream where the waiter asked me if I had any mail because they needed some. However, I must admit, I'm still waiting for the Womanhood Knowledge-stuff that was supposed to happen after I lost my virginity.

I rode into San Francisco and everone in the city seemed to be like, *HEY! HEY! LOOK AT ME!* and you want to look, too, so they'll look at you when it's your turn./quid pro quo./San Francisco felt like a seventies musical where there's enough room for everyone to jump off park statues singing and feel famous, loved, and remembered for a while.

There was the feeling that New York's more fragile freaks had moved to San Francisco to be in the sun and feel alive and special. It's virtually impossible to feel special in New York—if you're anything less than president of the United States or Bette Midler, you're nothing more than a frantic cockroach.

I rode down the extremely young and garishly heterosexual Haight Street, to the edge of Golden Gate Park. That's where white kids go to pick their scabs and pretend they're poor. Old homeless black guys ask them for their money because they sense their liberal white guilt. I shopped for food at the grocery store there and dropped all my clothes into a huge washing machine next door. There was a tired-looking old lady who walked around with a mop as if it were a cane, and she let me clean myself up at a wash sink in the back.

White people in dreadlocks: Even now, the concept DRAGS itself into my head kicking and screaming.

I sat outside on a bench and continued watching white kids in dreadlocks pretend they were disadvantaged artists with groundbreaking ideas. But their posture and teeth were too straight and white to fool anyone who's accepted donated bras in junior high.

I put my laundry in the dryer and sat back on the bench eating sourdough bread and cheddar cheese, and wondered why I couldn't really see the sequins of humanity and fall madly in love with the human race.

We burn people alive and try to hang them at the same time, we rip the fingernails and ovaries out of eighty-year-old women with knives and make them watch as we rape their grandchildren. Suburban kids torture animals on their living room floors and we put cats to sleep if they don't match the carpeting. I cannot imagine having a kid that might have to go to war and get his legs blown off one day. Why are concentration camps such a surprise? My only surprise is that they're not on every other corner like 7-11 stores. And if you think your peers don't have it in them to ignore the tortured sounds of Prometheus's liver being ripped out every day, watch a pissed-off roommate move out. It can be one of the scariest things you'll ever see.

And the possibility of being reincarnated and being dropped in a future Auschwitz really makes me want to hang onto some kind of spiritual door jamb.

The trip was over and here I was, hardly any different. Instead of sitting on the laundromat bench emanating love and strength, I felt like the kind of cranky old man neighborhood kids tell monster stories about.

Where the fuck was I supposed to be? I never got what I was looking for or where I was looking to go. I wasn't a good blue-collar heterosexual in a trailer home. I wasn't a real Puerto Rican in the Bronx. I wasn't a good one-night-stand lesbian. I wasn't a good alcoholic artist, and I wasn't a real biker chick because I didn't want the tattoos./Have you ever seen an old person with a tattoo?

← grandpa's mermaid tattoo from 1938

chapter forty-two
Is This ALL ThERE Is
and
D I V E R S I O N

No longer satisfied with the quiet bliss of my own company. I wanted (sex for some other reason) something different. someone smart. right away. I wanted to immediately (have sex for some other reason) fall in love with someone I both pitied and was impressed by. Someone who could give me answers / (sex for some other reason with) someone who appeared to have more problems than myself. There's not much room for respect in (sex for some other reason) an arrangement like that. but it works because you feel needed and turned on by their incompetence/competence at the same time. Like when it's time to leave, you can pull out the reason why like an ace up your sleeve. and saunter out the door.

Trouble is. you think you're walking away with spurs hitting a hardwood floor. but you've got spinach in your teeth. your skirt tucked in your underwear, and toilet paper on the bottom of your shoe. Yeah, the older I got, the harder it got to fuck someone worthy of my disrespect.

I wasn't the type to risk getting in a relationship with someone who insisted on dragging all my quirks out into the middle of the street so they could be run over to death by neo-postmodern analytical bullshit. Forward, reverse, and forward again, until everything that they liked in the first place, is nothing but Tabasco road kill. Back to road kill/even in Love.

Sitting on the bench outside the laundromat, I saw the threshold go up as I was unimpressed with guys who swaggered away from their bikes two blocks from home to buy a pack of cigarettes. Big deal. A month earlier, I would've creamed myself just knowing they owned leather jackets.

I pulled my laundry out of the dryer, changed into some warm fresh jeans and a sweatshirt in the back room. Then I rolled the rest of the clothes back up and stuffed them into my saddlebags. I called Hodie up to tell her I made it to San Francisco and was on my way over to her Sex Toy office.

If I couldn't leave Philadelphia with a tear-stained woman behind waving bye to me with a dishtowel, I wanted at least to ride up to one in San Francisco. Not caring whoever she was, I wanted to ride up to her smiling, shiny, and clean without road grime caked around my nostrils, black grit in my ears, the dead layer of my skin sloughed off, smelling fresh and clean like fabric softener and unreality.

I figured I'd have to go back into the motorcyle-rider fantasy to bring people into my joy at really standing alone, anywhere / for the first time.

So I went back into the grocery store to buy cheap burgundy lipstick. I applied it in front of the plastic wavy mirror on top of an eyeglass rack near the entrance and carefully wedged my helmet back over my head like a big heel in a very small shoe.

Feeling very sexy with cheap burgundy lipstick on, I walked out of the store squeezing my own butt. I made a whole ceremony of swinging my leg over the bike, past my out-of-state tags, over my April-fresh clothes in the saddlebags.

I ground my crotch into the seat so my labia could settle in the little groove it'd made for itself after so many miles, and I turned my key in the ignition.

But my bike wouldn't start / still wouldn't start again.

And it really, really wasn't gonna start, so I called Hodie and asked how to take the bus to her office.

The bus smelled entirely of urine, but I considered myself very lucky because I sat next to a man who smelled like the chopped spaghetti they used to serve in grade school.

"Hey, hey you gotta quarter?" he asked.

I reached into my pocket and came out with a dollar.

"No, no, no," he said. "I really do mean a quarter. I've gotta make a phone call."

"A phone call?" I asked.

"Yeah."

"Okay, wait a minute," I said. I reached into every teeny tiny pocket I had and finally came out with a quarter and a lot of lint bunched up under my fingernails. "Oh, and you should use one of these on the earpiece." I handed him a clean fast-food napkin so he wouldn't get any public ear grunge on himself.

"You sure are thoughtful," he smiled and nodded to me.

Then out of the blue, just like *that*, I asked him what he thought about death. He said we're like the plants in the park. Some are in bloom, some are buds, and then they die. New ones come. It was so simple, made so much sense. I started to feel better. But like most nice thoughts in my head, they usually only last for a little while like ice cream in my stomach/smoke in my lungs. Then the Stephen King worms crawl back around my future dead eyes and I'm afraid again of how unpretty it all becomes.

But what he said felt too simple and true to be bullshit, and I wanted to find the beauty in road kill. Like, if ideas could be compared to styles, what he said would be solid, simple Scandinavian wood furniture, while a lot of New Age stuff could be compared to frilly, cheesy fiberboard Spanish-style furniture with woodgrain paper pasted on top.

I hope the Scandinavian furniture feeling stays with me. I realize there isn't going to be One Answer. There are going to be a whole lot of little ones I have to collect maybe forever. Like a Danish desk here, a Swedish chair over there, and finally a Norwegian telephone to tell me what's going on.

I saw the corner where I was supposed to get off. I said bye and thanks so much. I said, so much you can't even know.

And by the time I walked up to Hodie's office an hour and two transfers later, I smelled like the spaghetti-urine bus and I could actually *feel* the burgundy lipstick fade and collect in the tiny lines of my mouth.

Zen again.

chApter Forty-thRee
Titty-Pink

Oh my God. Lots of California Merlot last night, and Hodie fucked me way before the science of pity, envy, and respect got to punch in the time clock. Forty-five years old with slicked-back short gray hair, she was like a queen lesbian going 120 miles an hour down hill without one iota of hesitation about turning on a somewhat straight girl.

She pulled off her long underwear shirt and had the kind of tits that deserved applause/no-pencil-holding tits with Bazooka gum nipples. So I thought she needed the regal title, "Hooter *Mujer*."

We lost time in long kisses./My favorite thing in the whole world. And I'd just gotten through explaining that it might take me a couple of times before I'd really feel comfortable enough to really get off. She didn't say anything / just laughed, closed her eyes, dropped her face a little deeper in my neck, and her hair was in my mouth, covering my eyes. It was like a big picture of squinting through your own wet eyelashes. Dragonfly wings up close.

Breathing so close to my ear she sounded like a Trans Am princess, and I knew then why everyone loved women or wanted to be one. My shirt was gone like a hairline and she made dandelion wishes / twisted my nipples with her fingers as if they were hers and she was going somewhere / slid my left leg out of her way, moved like a French kiss and took me to Coney Island.

She proved me a liar like real fast, and it took me time to come back, wipe the mustard from my lips and do simple things like walk across the room.

I proudly rubbed my sore pubic bone all the time, and wondered if I'd started a callus or something. Did lesbians have callused pubic bones the way school kids have calluses from holding pencils?

Fingers curved in the shape of a letter C can do things like actually *move* and tickle parts of you you've only read about and vaguely remember where they are. And after years of quietly bitching about the dirty sheets men have left behind, and thinking women fucking each other had to be the driest game in town, I learned I'm actually one of those female ejaculators I used to read about. See? It's like when you make faces and your face stays like that when you get old, so you'd better be careful.

At first, it was embarrassing leaving involuntary wet spots all over the bed. Hooter *Mujer* noticed it first. I thought I just wet myself, but she got all happy, bared her teeth, and just plowed right back inside me with a growling sound. While she was fucking me, I'd keep trying to reach for a sock, a shirt,

249

or a pair of underwear so I could place it over different spots, but she finally got what I was doing and told me to stop it. I said no. That before I knew it, I'd be squirting on everyone's furniture to mark my territory.

Anyway, fucking your dad's business partner has got to be the closest thing to working out the Electra complex, but it becomes an Oedipal blender drink when you figure I wouldn't get my mouth off of her nipples all night. They were fantastic like titty-pink toothpaste caps. It took her a long time to do things like answer the phone or do the dishes that way, but she was a good sport.

And I didn't care that she drank enough to qualify for a volume discount at the liquor store; she took away my fear of road kill and the future. Being with Hodie made me think less and that was good. She was a simple woman. The kind of woman who said "nothing" when you asked her what she was thinking. She was the kind of woman who worried about lead in her water and the fat content of her ice cream, but drank enough whiskey to make her liver beg for mercy in the English language. She was a hard-core professional at having a good time—decades of heroin, cocaine, and alcohol had given her a fluttery short-circuit look in her eyes that told you not to wing anything too complicated at her.

Do you know how it is when an animal chews halfway through a phone cord, and you hear sputtering static until you move it around? Well, that's how it was falling in love with a big yellow meat dog who'd chased too many balls outside fifth-floor windows.

I figured if things got serious between us, I could spend my youth trying to save her, and when that wouldn't work, go to Al-Anon meetings for the rest of my life.

wahoo / yeeha.

To my relief, the next morning I didn't feel like a member of a lesbian gang. I didn't feel this urge to subscribe to lesbian magazines, wear flannel shirts, wave DOWN WITH THE PATRIARCHY signs in the air, or watch bad lesbian movies to see myself represented. No.

I wanted a Bisexual Female Ejaculating Quaker role model. And where was she, dammit? From now on I would demand to be represented.

  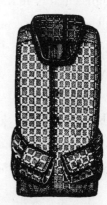

chapter forty-four

Messages From the Little Ant-People

We were in bed and Hodie was on the phone with her father in Galveston, Texas. She'd said everyone got brain cancer there, and was kind of figuring she'd probably get it, too. Then she lit a cigarette so she'd be wrong. I lit one too, so we'd be wrong together.

I was watching one of those British mysteries I love on public television. English actors talk faster than Puerto Rican housewives, so I always have one hell of a time keeping up. But it's easy to catch on because their murders happen in the last twenty minutes, after forty minutes of intense character development.

The mystery had just begun, so I had plenty of time to stare at a little trail of ants that lead to the empty pint of ice cream I'd polished off. And then I heard tiny little voices going, *hey, hey, over here*. I was getting a special little message from the ants. Here's what they told me: They said that the cult of personality fakes you out/makes you think some people have sweeter-smelling craps. That maybe you think your craps can smell a special way if you get enough attention. But, ha ha, individuality is way overrated because you are a part of the earth just like everything else, and if you die trying to deny it by getting a lead-lined casket, you would just turn into creepy, disgusting, isolated slime. Be humble and realize you're no better than any of the worms, the trees, or the little man who picked his nose in the back of your class. You're not so special! Rot proudly and be one with the earth!

I whispered thanks to the ants and then I just heard a lot of British actors insinuating things to each other on public television. Being told by the ants that I wasn't so special, and to rot proudly and be one with the earth made me feel more peaceful. It was the antithesis of everything I'd learned from art openings in the 1980s. Even though we die alone, I was beginning to think this whole individuality thing was a crock. Secretaries in cubicles just may be real gurus.

Back to the Jell-O theory of individuality where I still don't know how much to be alone and together.

Hodie hung up the phone—and like *that*—I stopped thinking.

Chapter Forty-Five
Flaming Postal Fantasies

"Eight hundred bucks? You're kidding!" I was talking on the phone to the mechanic who'd towed my bike to her shop in the back of a pickup truck, and she was telling me I had a burnt valve. I wanted to tell her how I was now a card-carrying member of the lesbian gang and she should give me a flannel-shirt break. There had to be privileges to breaking on through to the other side.

But instead I got off the phone and lit a cigarette because I just didn't have the money, and I doubted she'd be as impressed as I was at finally being a lesbian.

I told Hodie I was going to have to start charging her for sex, but she just laughed and pulled the fat-free ice cream out of the freezer. Six feet tall, 140 pounds, and *she* had the nerve to pull fat-free ice cream out of the freezer and

say, "Darlin', you just think you're the funniest thing since split cookies."
There was that southern bullfrog's-butt-so-low-to-the-ground kind of talk.

I asked her what split cookies were and why they were supposed to be so
damn funny, but she didn't know. One thing I did know, however, was that
she wasn't taking my shot at being a lesbian hooker seriously. Maybe because
all I did was lay there. I was a brand-new lesbian, and I still didn't know
what I was doing. I felt like a virgin all over again, as if the last two dozen
years hadn't been fresh enough. I was intimidated and I hated to be afraid of
anything, especially another woman's pussy. My hand felt like a little fly
hovering over her clitoris whenever I touched her, and the last time I tried to
fuck her, I turned my hand the wrong way at a crucial moment and hurt her.
It made me feel like a bad man.

I thought about her fingers and realized I should be paying her.

Hooter ate tiny little amounts of food as if she were on a commercial airline.
She took a spoon of ice cream, put it in a bowl, and took one bite before
saying she was full. She put it back in what she called the "ice box" and lit a
cigarette, then asked me, "Why don't you come and work with me for a little
while, darlin'?"

"As your secretary?" I asked with a hint of *no-fucking-way* in my voice.

"No. Your dad said you were a really good artist, and well, this may be strange, but I've been thinking it would be good for us to branch out beyond lavender dolphin dildos, and do something a little different. Make us stand out in the market, you know?"

"You mean you want me to come up with a new line of dildos?" The modern day Electra complex was playing itself out more elegantly than I could've ever imagined. And I'd be able to pay for my bike with penis money.

Yeah.

I excused myself to take a shower and think about it. I always got my best ideas in the shower.

The more I thought about it, the more I got all these ideas about penises—no more cutesy aquatic mammal dildos. They would be groundbreaking penises. Fake penis magnets for the outside of your car. . . penis ashtrays for cigars that were just cigars, multipurpose penises for those who lived in the cities and had very little space—the Swiss Army Penis.

I could do a complete art show around them, and have huge art openings at big galleries all over America and Muslim countries. I could promote the summer line of fake penises on talk shows, but appear in disguise, so that I wouldn't be recognized later on the beach while designing the new winter fake penises. We could sell the less expensive velour penises late at night on the shopping channel and we'll never say "cheaper." There'd even be fake penis catalogues for those living in more remote parts of the world. I could make motivational penis tapes and CDs and say things like *I don't know about you, but I care about you—what are you waiting for—you can buy an entire penis now now now with no money down—let me show you how—you work hard and deserve a break with our special fake penis frozen dinners and wash it down with our brand-new fake penis colas/yes.*

And just in case you blinked when the whole thing started, there'd be a best-selling biography on the trials and tribulations of the fake penises, inspirational fake penis stories of phony tragedy, pretend revenge, make-believe love, and counterfeit impotence.

Yes! And then the U.S. postal people would call me up at home and ask me if I could do a series of fake penis first-class postage stamps for them, and I would either say, "ladies, stop wearing those unflattering pants, you have gashes on your hips" or more likely, "what a perfect combination!" because fake penises and postage stamps are all about penetration, communication, and dreams coming true in front of warped circus mirrors for EVERYBODY.

La La La.

THE
End

Let's Pretend this was a MOVIE and these are THE CRedits at The End

First, I'd like to thank my mom, Debby, and my sister, Elena, for being okay with never having any privacy. You both put up with all those existential anxieties I never quite grow out of. Thanks for saying smart things and making me giggle until my face hurts, my stomach aches, my throat is raw, my lungs are clear, and life is better. And thanks to my second mom, Cat, who makes the best meatballs in the galaxy./She's so tough, she smokes Tampax.

Thanks to glamorous Kelly Yon for teaching me how to ride a rental scooter at the last minute.

And thanks to Ivan Leibowitz for simply giving me your bike just like (snap) that.

Thanks, Mister Mark Lammers for letting me steal all your jokes. Thanks for the long rides where we'd philosophize and binge on fat-free frozen yogurt and cigarettes in your luxury car, and thanks for letting me use your office to write, even though I often made your staff very nervous. Come to think of it, what could you have possibly gotten out of this relationship?

Thanks to Sandra May for the longest relationship I've ever had over a month. You found my G-spot and gave me orgasms that made me cry. You've been my lifeline during this last agoraphobic year-and-a-half, wiping the grime off my face and doing the dishes that would've still been in the sink today if it hadn't been for you. Good luck, Lady May, and don't forget to make that pussy-mashing porn movie. What the world needs now is not love, sweet love, no—it needs decent lesbian porn. Hurry up: I've got the VCR remote in my hand and a case of batteries under my feet.

Thanks to Emily Charles: Even though you're the definition of cool, you brainstorm like the jitterbug. Thanks for being stark-nakedly honest and helping me to always come up with something better.

Thanks to Mary Starvis, my upstairs neighbor, for not vacuuming after 11 P.M. You make me laugh until I spit your divine omelettes out my nose.

Thanks to the Pennsylvania Council of the Arts and the Ludwig
Vogelstein Foundation: You. you lit up my life/you gave me hope to
carry on.

Thanks to Leigh Feldman. The Great Warrior Princess Agent with
machete-wit and frontal cleavage. Hercules and Xena are her friends/they
drop by her office for lunch. so don't be coy with her. /Leigh. I'm so glad
you're not one of those pretentious. jogging. bulimic New York agents
I've heard scary stories about. I dare say that it is because of you that I'm
not out murdering retail managers. and I feel a strong business-like love
for you because of it./I salute you with the war cry of The Great
Warrior Princess Agent in action:
"Ay ay ay ay ay! "

And my editor. Bob Mecoy: Thanks for all the long-distance therapy over
the phone during the highest rates of the day. You never even bitched
about it cutting into your project budget. You're beyond swell./Bravo.
Bob. Working with you has been a fucking breeze/a zephyr/a nasal
whistle that sounds like a bunch of nuns singing hymns. So I have
decided that you are my creative guru. and I will follow you around like
a big yellow meat dog until you drop me off in the woods and drive away
real fast. You're brilliant. forceful. and butch—and since you also look
good in a suit. whatever you're making. it's not enough. Demand more.
Much more. Bob.

Thanks to Sweet Pete Fornatale. It's amazing how you return calls even before they're made and thanks for picking up where Papa Bob leaves off. You've got a secretly wicked sense of humor and you'd make a good black man. And like me, you also know that Nancy Drew was really a black man.

Thanks to Belinda Batcha at Signature Software for putting up with my personal font obsessions.

Thanks to the extremely generous rubber stamp people who, in the spirit of creativity said, "Sure, you can use some of my stuff, no problem": Lynette Wagner, "Our Lady of Rubber"; and Miss Moneypenny at "100 Proof Press."

And I'd also like to thank Bill Rosen (the alpha dog/the visionary/the man who ultimately took away my fake penis endpapers); Marla Stutman (my peppy printing hero); Paul Smith and Michael Accordino (shiny silver art boys); and Maria Massey and David Frost (the *amazing* human-flea-comb copy editors who know ABSOLUTELY EVERYTHING) at Simon & Schuster. You all made this a cool-looking book and now it's like we're in a special gang. A special gang bonded together by our anal-retentive creativity. /Let's make Bill Rosen the leader and talk about his butt whenever he walks away for a cigarette./Hey, thanks---every last one of you deserves a great big sweaty bear hug. The kind of hug I suspect Bill might give after a day of saying NO to everyone else's fake penis endpapers. /Thanks again for making this project more fun than going to a whorehouse with a box full of whoopee cushions.

And now if you'll excuse me, I'm going to go out and buy myself a crystal jelly G-spot vibrator.

Wahoo.

AFTER